JOSIE

MARGERY SCOTT

MAIL-ORDER BRIDES OF SAPPHIRE SPRINGS

Miranda
Audra
Kathryn
Elise

OTHER HISTORICAL ROMANCES

Emma's Wish
Wild Wyoming Wind
Rose: Bride of Colorado

MEDICAL ROMANCES

The Surgeon's Homecoming
Stranded with the Surgeon
The Firefighter and the Lady Doc

CONTEMPORARY ROMANCES

Winterlude

CHAPTER 1

Chicago, 1880

Josie Parker's heartbeat stuttered at the news. "But I have nowhere to go."

Mrs. Norton, the woman in charge of the Good Samaritan Children's Home, peered at her over the top of her spectacles which always sat near the end of her nose. Josie had wondered sometimes how the woman managed to keep them from falling off, but in the years she'd been at the orphanage in Chicago, she'd never seen it happen.

"I'm sorry, Josephine," Mrs. Norton said, "but you know those are the rules. You can't stay here once you're eighteen, and that will be in two weeks. I assumed you'd already made plans for your future."

The sympathy in Mrs. Norton's voice undid her. Tears welled up in her eyes. "No," she sputtered. "I ... I kept hoping there was some way I could stay here ... I've never lived anywhere but here ..."

"That's not possible, dear. There are so many young children who need care that we can't allow grown women to take up the space."

"I ... I don't know what to do," she muttered. "I don't really know how to do anything."

Mrs. Norton got up and rounded her desk to sit in the chair beside Josie's. She took her hand. "You're a smart girl," she said. "You can cook, you can sew, and even though I disapproved, you have skills very few women have. Although where you'd be permitted to use them, I don't know," she added with a short chuckle.

That much was true, Josie thought. She would be a good wife one day, even if she did prefer doing "man's work." She'd spent so much time with Hank, the orphanage's handyman, that he'd come to rely on her for help over the years. He'd taught her how to build furniture, how to repair a leaky roof and she'd even worked alongside him to put in the pipes to bring water into the house so they didn't have to go outside in the middle of winter to fetch water from the well.

None of that would be of any use now, though. It was highly unlikely she'd find that kind of employment anywhere in Chicago. Just a few months before, her best friend, Sally, had left the orphanage and hadn't been able to find work. She'd come back to visit a few times since then and had told her what she was doing to survive. It had made Josie cringe at the thought.

Josie had found that when reality was too painful to

deal with, she could distance herself by focusing on something else. She needed to do that now.

She slid a glance at the painting on the wall behind Mrs. Norton's desk. Majestic mountains rose into a bright blue sky. "Where is that, Mrs. Norton?" she asked. "It's so beautiful."

"I believe that particular scene is in Montana."

"I'd like to see the mountains in person one day. And the ocean … and the Pyramids … and Paris, and …"

"Josephine!" Mrs. Norton's voice interrupted Josie's wayward thoughts.

"Sorry, I just …"

"There is one other solution, if you're willing."

Josie was willing to do just about anything, since the only future she saw for herself was the same as Sally's, selling herself at one of the brothels near the waterfront. "What is it?"

"An acquaintance of mine runs an agency," Mrs. Norton began.

"An employment agency?"

Mrs. Norton shook her head. "Not exactly. It's a matrimonial agency," she went on. "Men in the west are anxious to marry, but there aren't enough women there so she arranges marriages for them."

Josie was intrigued. "Out west?" That would mean she'd be able to travel, to see some of the country outside Chicago.

"Yes. Of course, you'd be expected to cook and clean and take care of your husband, and to … to perform your wifely duties," she went on. "All of them."

While Sally had told her what happened between men and women and how babies came to be, she'd never gone into detail. Josie had been aghast at the few descriptions Sally had offered, and she couldn't imagine why any woman would marry and willingly subject herself to such treatment.

"In return," Mrs. Norton went on, "you would have a home and eventually, children."

A home of her own. Josie had never known her family, and her only home had been the orphanage for as far back as she could remember.

She would have to submit to her husband, but surely submitting to one man would be better than submitting to a different man every night—or more than one man, if what Sally told her was true.

The words stuck in Josie's throat, but she couldn't see any other options. "I'll do it."

"Wonderful." Mrs. Norton rose. "I'll get in touch with Mrs. Stuart immediately and make arrangements for you to go and see her. I'm sure she'll be able to find you the perfect husband."

Josie's knees quaked more than Mr. Kalinack's newborn colt's as she climbed the stairs to the second floor of the brick office building in downtown Chicago a few days later. She'd had to walk for three miles to reach the matrimonial agency, and even though she was used to exercise, her feet ached and perspiration trickled down her back.

She'd never been so far away from the orphanage before, but Mrs. Norton's directions had made the building easy to find.

A long corridor stretched out in both directions when she reached the top of the stairs. Not knowing which way to go, she silently recited a rhyme which always helped her decide between two options. She turned to the right and slowly walked down the corridor, pausing to read the sign on each door.

Near the end of the corridor, she found the door she'd been looking for—*Stuart Matrimonial Agency.*

She tucked a few strands of her blonde hair that had come loose from her hairpins under her hat. She ran her hands down the skirt of her green cotton Sunday dress to smooth out any wrinkles and dislodge any dust from her long walk to reach downtown. The dress was well-worn and didn't fit properly, but it was the best she had, so it would have to do.

Then, taking in a deep breath, she opened the door and stepped inside.

A woman with grey-streaked hair was sitting at a large wooden desk. She waved Josie to a chair facing her. "My name is Helen Stuart," she said with a smile. "You're Josephine Parker, I presume."

Josie detected a slight accent in the woman's voice. Scottish? Irish? She didn't know, and really, it didn't matter. At least the woman seemed friendly enough, but Josie's throat was so dry she couldn't speak. She nodded.

"Mrs. Norton told me you'd like to become a mail-order bride, preferably somewhere in the mountains," the woman said, sliding a sheet of paper across the desk toward Josie. "I do have a husband for you in Montana if you're willing."

Josie's heart hammered in her chest. "I am," she squeaked.

"Good. Read his letter and if you still agree, you can write to him and tell him when you'll be arriving. He has already sent a train ticket as well as stagecoach fare and he'd like a bride as soon as possible.

Dear future bride,

My name is Cooper Thompson and I live in Coldwater Creek, Montana.

I'm looking for a bride who's young and able to handle life on a cattle ranch. My brother and his little boy live on the ranch, too, and it would be nice if you could help with them as well.

I'm 23 and I have black hair and blue eyes. I'm 5'10" so I'd like a woman who's shorter than me but not by a whole lot.

I promise that if you marry me, I'll look after you and you'll never have to worry about money or safety. I admit I do get grumpy when I'm tired and maybe it's not smart to tell a woman my faults, but I think it's important to be honest. I have other faults, too, but I'm not a big drinker, I don't gamble and I treat women with respect.

I'd really like to get married before winter sets in, so if you think you'd like to take a chance and marry me, I'm

*enclosing a train ticket and stagecoach fare to Coldwater
Creek.*

Yours truly,
Cooper Thompson

Less than a half hour later, Josie left Mrs. Stuart's office,
her head spinning. She was now betrothed to a man
more than a thousand miles away and she'd be leaving
Chicago and everybody she'd ever known in six days.

As she began the long walk back to the orphanage,
tears filled her eyes. In less than a month, she'd be leaving
everything and everyone she'd ever known.

Six weeks later, Josie carefully descended the stagecoach
steps in Coldwater Creek, Montana. The driver set her
small trunk beside her, tipped his hat and strolled away.

What she'd expected the town to look like, she
couldn't say. She did know this wasn't it. False-fronted
shops and businesses lined both sides of a dirt street.
Men in wagons and on horseback rode by, while only a
few women hurried about, intent on their errands.

A soft smile tugged at her lips. It seemed Mrs.
Norton had been right when she'd told Josie that
men far outnumbered women in the west. Before
Josie had left Chicago, she'd asked Sally to come with
her. Sally had tearfully refused, pointing out that
since she was in debt to Gus Angstrom, the owner of

the brothel, she was too afraid of what he'd do to her if she left. Sally had begged Josie to write, wished her well, and promised that one day, they'd see each other again.

Josie glanced around, her gaze searching for the man she was supposed to marry. Where was he? Surely he intended to meet her, didn't he? If this was how he planned to treat her, she'd soon find herself another man to marry instead, since the woman at the matrimonial agency had assured her she'd have her pick of men in Montana.

She didn't pay much attention to the young woman walking toward her. She looked to be about Josie's age, and was wearing a robin's-egg blue dress dotted with white flowers and a matching blue feathery hat perched on her ebony hair.

Josie turned away to avoid staring, expecting the woman to pass her and continue on her way.

"Miss Parker?"

Josie spun around to face the woman. "Yes," she replied, returning her smile and noticing her dark blue eyes for the first time.

"I'm Nora Thompson," she said. "Cooper's sister."

"I'm pleased to meet you, Miss Thompson," Josie said, holding out her hand.

The woman took it. "Please, call me Nora since we're going to be family. May I call you Josephine?"

"If you must," she replied with a wry grin, "but most people call me Josie."

"Then Josie it is."

Josie's gaze wandered to the street around them. "Where is Cooper? Has something happened to him?"

Nora's smile faded. "No, no. He's fine."

"I expected him to come and meet me—"

"Yes … well, that's why … I mean there's something I need to tell you."

Josie's stomach lurched. Whenever someone said those words, it was never good news.

Nora took a step toward a bench against the wall in front of the Wells Fargo office. "Please, let's sit down and I'll explain."

Josie followed her and perched on the edge of the bench. She set her reticule on her lap and clasped her hands together on top. "What is it?"

"I have a confession to make," Nora began. A flush crept into her cheeks. "Cooper didn't write the letter to the matrimonial agency. I did."

Josie sucked in a breath. Her fingers flew to her lips. "What?"

"I'm sorry," Nora said.

"But … but he knows you wrote it, doesn't he?"

"Well … not exactly. I did tell him he should get a mail-order bride because I wouldn't be around forever, and he didn't refuse."

"But he didn't agree either, I assume."

Nora shook her head.

Josie's heart skipped a beat as the reality of the situation she'd found herself in hit her. The man she expected to marry didn't even know she existed.

"I don't understand. Why would you do such a thing?"

At least Nora had the decency to look contrite. "I shouldn't have. I know that. But Cooper needs a wife. And Drew and Andy—"

"Wait!" Josie was getting more confused by the second. "Who are Drew and Andy?"

A slow flush colored Nora's cheeks. "I ... forgot to mention them ..."

Josie didn't like the sound of that. Things were going from bad to worse. "And they are?"

"Drew is our brother, and Andy is Drew's little boy. He's only four."

"What do they have to do with any of this?"

"Well ..." Nora's voice lowered to barely more than a whisper. "They live at the ranch, too."

Josie bounded to her feet and took a few steps before spinning around. Planting her hands on her hips, she glared at Nora. "So not only was I tricked into coming here to marry Cooper, I was expected to take care of his brother and his nephew, too?"

"I'm sorry ..."

"Sorry doesn't help," Josie sputtered. "What in Heaven's name possessed you to do this?"

"I took care of Cooper after our parents were killed three years ago. Drew was already married and was living in Wyoming. I cooked for Cooper, I cleaned for him, I did his laundry. Then when Drew's wife died, he didn't handle it well. Cooper persuaded him to bring Andy to Coldwater Creek. He built a house near ours and he and Andy live there, but they eat their meals with Cooper and I. I look after Andy when Cooper and Drew are working the ranch. I love them all dearly, but it's time for me to live my own life."

Josie hated to admit it, but she did understand how Nora must feel. Still ...

"Lewis Grimsby has been courting me for some time," Nora went on. "He wants to marry me and I want to marry him."

It was all starting to make sense now. Nora was looking for someone to take her place.

"Surely your brothers are capable of taking care of themselves," Josie interjected.

"If it was just them, I would let them walk around naked and starve until they figured out how to look after themselves, but I can't leave Andy with them. He's too young to look out for himself, and he needs a woman's care."

"Then wouldn't it make more sense for Drew to get married again since it's his son who needs looking after?"

"It would," Nora agreed, "but he's not ready to think about that yet. It's only been a year and he's still grieving."

"I see."

"I thought if I could find Cooper a wife to take care of them, I could marry Lewis, and I wouldn't feel guilty for leaving. It was wrong. I know that now."

"It most certainly was," Josie snapped. Still, Nora's reasoning did make sense. A four-year-old couldn't take care of himself.

Josie really didn't know what she would have done

herself in the same situation. She could understand that it would seem like the perfect solution to Nora.

"When you wrote and said you were an orphan," Nora said, "I thought you might like to have a family."

Yes, she wanted a family. She'd wished and hoped and prayed for a family of her own for years until finally, she'd given up. It had never occurred to her that she'd be walking into a ready-made family when she'd agreed to marry Cooper Thompson.

"Do you have the fare for me to get back to Chicago?" Josie asked.

A flush crept into Nora's cheeks. "I'm sorry. I spent all my savings to pay your fare here."

Josie couldn't believe what she was hearing. She had a few dollars, but not nearly enough to get home. Not that she had a home to go back to anyway, she reminded herself.

She spun around, searching for the stagecoach. It was gone. "When's the next stage?"

A flush crept into Nora's cheeks. "It comes through here once a week."

"What am I supposed to do in the meantime? I don't have the money to get back to Chicago and I don't have enough money to stay in a hotel until the stage comes back."

Nora lowered her head, avoiding Josie's gaze. "I didn't think … I really am sorry."

The woman sounded as if she was going to burst into tears at any moment, and for some reason Josie didn't understand herself, some of her anger washed away.

She knew how easy it was to impulsively make a decision without taking the time to really consider the consequences. Hadn't she done exactly the same thing by agreeing to marry a man she'd never seen, in a town hundreds of miles from everything she'd ever known?

She couldn't really find fault with Nora's actions. She'd had a good reason for what she'd done, and it showed she loved her family very much.

But Josie was still left with a situation she had no way to deal with.

Her gaze scanned the street. Was there somewhere here in this town where she might earn a living besides the saloon? How could she lower herself to—?

"You can stay with us at the ranch." Nora's voice interrupted Josie's thoughts. "The house is plenty big enough and I know once I explain to Cooper that it's my fault you're here and why I sent for you, he'll see marrying you is the right thing to do. You're much prettier than I expected and I'm sure he'll think so, too. He won't turn you down."

"And if he does?"

Nora got to her feet. "Let's worry about that if it happens."

When it happens, Josie muttered under her breath.

Nora glanced around. "Where are your trunks?"

"I only have one," Josie replied.

"Then let's get it loaded into the wagon and we'll head back to the ranch."

Josie wanted to refuse, but she couldn't see she had any other choice but to go with this woman and hope her brother wanted a wife. If he didn't ... No, she wouldn't think about that until she had to.

A few minutes later, her trunk was stowed in the bed of the wagon and Josie was sitting beside Nora on the seat.

"The ranch isn't far," Nora commented, flicking the reins. The wagon began to move and soon they'd left Coldwater Creek behind. Josie couldn't help thinking about the man she was going to, a man who had no idea his life was about to be turned upside down.

CHAPTER 2

*C*ooper Thompson stood on the roof and smiled as his gaze swept the pastures around the farmhouse.

In the distance, the foothills rose in purple and green to the majestic mountains reaching into the sky. Even now, with the summer sun shining in the cloudless blue sky, there were still patches of snow on the highest peaks.

The mountains never ceased to amaze him, and he was thankful every day that he'd bought this piece of land four years before.

The ranch wasn't the biggest in the territory by any means, but it was plenty big enough for him and his family. It provided a good living for them all, and he even had some money put away to add on to the house if he ever wanted to.

There was no reason to ever add rooms to the house,

though. Why would he? He had no intention of ever marrying. He'd seen over and over again how loving a woman left a man either miserable or heartbroken. Men who fell in love were fools. That was all there was to it. And he was no fool.

He could use the money to expand the ranch, he supposed. But again, why? He was happy with what he had. He didn't need more money.

He and Drew took care of the ranch work and made sure Nora wanted for nothing. She, in turn, took care of the house and Andy during the day until Drew was finished the day's work.

He'd offered to hire a housekeeper to make Nora's life easier, but she'd refused. Even if they could find a woman willing to live away from town with two men, Nora always said nobody would look after the house and her family the way she could. She was probably right.

Lately, though, she'd been keeping company with Lewis Grimsby, and one of these days, he might want to marry her. Cooper didn't know what they'd do then, but he'd worry about it when the time came.

Right now, life was good.

He hadn't planned on spending the better part of the day fixing the leak in the barn roof that had sprung during the storm the night before, though. He'd have to fix the roof on the henhouse, too, one of these days. Still, when it came to hardships, this wasn't so bad.

The afternoon sun beat down. He took off his hat, wiped his brow with the sleeve of his shirt and set his hat back on his head. He lowered himself to his knees and set a nail in the new shingle. He was about to hammer it into place when movement out of the corner of his eye caught his attention.

He watched as a cloud of dust in the distance moved along the trail that ran along the river's edge. Must be Nora coming back, he mused, turning back to his task.

When he looked up again, the wagon had already left the trail and was passing by a stand of cedars near the border of his land. He squinted into the sun. Nora was driving, but she wasn't alone. A woman dressed in dark brown or black was sitting beside her.

He dropped the nails he'd been holding back into the paper sack and set the hammer down, then climbed down the ladder and waited until the wagon drew to a stop in front of him.

The woman sitting beside Nora looked up at him, her forehead creased in a frown. A dark blue bonnet covered her hair, but a few pale blond curls had escaped to frame her face. Wide greenish-gold eyes gazed up at him, studying him. The dress he'd thought was brown was actually dark blue and emphasized her creamy skin. All in all, she was one of the prettiest women he'd laid eyes on in quite some time.

He'd noticed a trunk in the wagon bed so he assumed whoever this woman was, she was here to stay for a while.

Nora climbed down out of the wagon. "Come with me, Cooper," she ordered, sliding her hand beneath his elbow. "We need to have a little talk."

"Aren't you going to introduce me to your friend?" he asked.

"Of course," she said. "Cooper, this is Josephine Parker. Josie, my brother, Cooper."

Josie held out her hand to shake Cooper's. He reached for her hand but then drew back. "Begging your pardon, ma'am, but my hands are dirty. Don't want to soil your gloves."

Josie smiled, but didn't lower her hand. "Mr. Thompson, I'm not the kind of woman who worries about a little dirt. I'm happy to meet you."

Cooper's lips creased in a smile. Tiny laugh lines appeared at the corners of his eyes, and he took her hand, burying it in his.

"Come on, Cooper." Nora tugged at Cooper's arm until he had no choice but to release Josie's hand and follow her away from the wagon toward the barn.

Josie stayed in the wagon, her eyes on Nora and her brother, her thoughts going back to her handshake with Cooper. Even through the fabric of her gloves, the way he'd held her hand had done something to her, a feeling unlike anything she'd ever felt before. It was most pleasant, but at the same time disturbing. She didn't like the unsettled sensation in her stomach and the warmth that seemed to radiate through her right to her toes.

She cast a glance at Nora and Cooper, now standing beside the barn. She hadn't noticed before how much

Nora used her hands to emphasize her words, but by the way they were waving around, she assumed the woman was having a hard time getting her point across.

Josie sat as primly as possible, her hands folded in her lap. Twice Cooper slid a look in her direction, his expression stormy. She quickly averted her gaze while heat of embarrassment flushed her cheeks.

She couldn't help noticing that even angry – which he appeared to be – he was a handsome man. Hair the color of coal, just like Nora's, deep blue eyes, a square chin and strong jaw.

The broad shoulders and muscled arms she'd seen were the result of hard labor, but at the same time, he wasn't built like the lumberjack she'd met once when he and his wife had come to the orphanage to visit a few years before.

Cooper looked at her again, and caught her gaze. She lowered her eyes. What must he be thinking of her?

She sneaked a peek at him, hoping he wasn't still looking at her. He was gazing out into the fields as he raked his fingers through his hair. Nora was standing quietly beside him, waiting.

Finally, he stopped and faced his sister. Josie couldn't tell what he was saying to Nora, but eventually he stopped talking.

Nora turned away from her brother and went up the stairs into the house, closing the door behind her.

For a few seconds, Cooper stared at Josie, then moved toward her. He stopped beside the wagon. "Seems Nora took it upon herself to find me a wife without telling me."

Josie nodded. "It does seem that way."

"Do you have the letters she wrote?" he asked. "I'd like to read them."

She reached into her reticule and pulled out a wrinkled envelope. "There was only one letter," she said, handing it to him.

He took the piece of paper out of the envelope. Josie watched his expression as he read it, his brows arching and his jaw tensing.

She felt that she needed to say something, anything, to break the silence. "I had no way of knowing you didn't write the letter yourself, although the handwriting did seem a bit feminine for a man, especially a rancher."

"You thought I was feminine and you still came all the way out here?"

She gave him a wry smile. "I thought the *handwriting* was feminine," she repeated. "The pressure was light, and the curlicues—"

"It wasn't mine," he interrupted.

"I know that now."

"So you came out here expecting to get married," he said quietly.

She nodded. She'd expected to be greeted by a man who'd sent for her, who wanted to marry her and raise a family with her.

"I'm not looking for a wife," he told her. "Nora had no business doing what she did."

"I agree," Josie said, "but it's done. The question is,

what do we do about it now? She tells me she doesn't have enough money to send me back to Chicago."

"I can pay your fare, if you want to go back. Do you want to?"

Josie thought for a minute, then shook her head. "I have nothing to go back to," she said, "but if you want me to leave, I'll go."

"What about your family?"

"I have none. I grew up in an orphanage."

"You don't talk like you came from an orphanage," he commented. "You sound like you went to one of those fancy finishing schools."

"Mrs. Norton, the matron of the orphanage, was determined we would be educated so that we'd have a better chance in life once we left."

"Why did you want to leave if you had nowhere else to go?"

"I didn't want to leave, but once I reached eighteen, I wasn't allowed to stay. I always wanted to see the mountains so when Mrs. Norton suggested becoming a mail-order bride, I agreed. She sent me to a friend of hers who runs a matrimonial agency. The letter she showed me was from Montana, and it felt like it was meant to be."

She still felt the same way, but she didn't think it was wise to say that.

His gaze shifted from her to the mountains. "Do the mountains live up to your expectations?"

Josie couldn't prevent the smile tugging at her lips. "Oh, yes. They're even more magnificent that I ever imagined."

He returned her smile, a few faint lines crinkling the corners of his eyes. Mercy, that smile …

"They really are," he said. "I can't imagine living anyplace where I can't look out on the mountains."

"So you can see why I came?"

His smile faded. "I do," he said. "And I'm really sorry Nora brought you here under false pretenses." He paused for a few moments as if he was trying to find the right words. "She wants to get married. Did she tell you that?"

Josie nodded.

"Did she also tell you she's not going to leave if I don't have somebody to look after the house … and us?"

That was a surprise to Josie. "No, she didn't," Josie replied. "And she also didn't tell me there was an "us" until we met this afternoon. I was under the impression I was marrying one man, not gaining an entire family."

He chuckled then, his eyes crinkling at the corners.

The anger Josie had been trying to quell rose up inside her. "I don't know why you think this is amusing, but I can assure you, it isn't. I've travelled hundreds of miles on the most uncomfortable seats you can imagine. I've eaten food I wouldn't feed to hogs, and I haven't had a proper bath in weeks, all to come here to marry a man I thought wanted me to become his wife, only to arrive and find out every word in that letter was a lie."

His smile faded, and a frown appeared between his eyes. "You're right, and I apologize. It really is nothing to laugh about, but sometimes, the only way to get through something unpleasant is to try to find humor in it."

"I have no money, no home and no way to make a

living. Please enlighten me and tell me where to find the humor in this situation."

Cooper met her gaze, his dark eyes studying her. Then he turned away and raked his fingers through his hair.

A hawk soared overhead, the screech breaking the silence that had settled over the land. Josie waited, unsure what she should do.

Finally, Cooper turned and closed the distance between them. "She's blackmailing me," he said. "She knows I'll do whatever I have to do to make her happy."

"Mr. Thompson—"

"You might as well start calling me Cooper since it looks like I have no choice but to marry you. If you're still willing, that is."

"Well, isn't that the most romantic proposal ever?" she asked, unable to hide the sarcasm in her voice.

His brows arched. "You were expecting romance?"

"Not really, but I wasn't expecting a proposal that sounded like it was only a little more appealing than a death sentence."

"Look," he said, jamming his hands in his pockets. "I don't need a wife. I don't want a wife. But I do want Nora to have a husband and children of her own. Drew and I could make do ourselves, but she's right about Andy needing a woman to look after him. So, I'm willing to marry you to make that happen. I'm not a romantic man so if that's the kind of man you expect, you'll be sorely disappointed. But I will provide for you and I won't mistreat you. That's all I'll promise to do. You said you have no home to go back to, so what do you say?"

Thoughts whirled frantically in Josie's brain. He apparently cared enough about his family that he was willing to sacrifice himself for his sister's happiness. Did that mean that as his wife, he'd do the same for her if he needed to? She hoped so, or at least that even if he didn't ever love her, he'd care about her well-being. And that was as much as she'd expected from a mail-order marriage.

She shifted on the seat, taking in the well-kept house, the sturdy barn, the fields. He took pride in his property. That was also a point in his favor.

She'd like to tell him she'd rather sleep in a ditch than marry a man who didn't want her, but common sense took over. She could do worse.

"It seems I have no other choice as well," she said softly. "I accept."

Cooper swung the hammer with more force than he needed to. The nail dug into the roof shingle and a moment later, the wood split. He swore.

The heat must have addled his brain, he thought. There couldn't be any other reason why he'd offered to marry a woman he'd met less than an hour ago.

Well, that and Nora's tears. He never could stand to see her cry, or any woman for that matter. It was the one weakness he'd admit to.

And Nora knew it. She'd used those tears more times than he could count over the years, and even though he did his best to harden himself against them, he'd never been able to.

So now, he was getting married to the woman he'd just watched climb the stairs and disappear into the house.

Not that she wasn't a pretty little thing. She was. She'd looked exhausted, but that wasn't surprising. He didn't know how long it took to get from Chicago to Coldwater Creek, but he knew it wasn't a short journey. For a man, it would be uncomfortable to be stuck in a stagecoach for days. For a woman, it would be so much worse.

Even though she wasn't all done up like the ladies in town, there was something about her that appealed to him. Wheat-colored curls had escaped from her bonnet and framed her face, emphasizing her pale skin and brownish eyes.

But she was small, likely not strong enough to deal with the hardships of ranch life. How would she ever handle all the work that would be expected of her?

At least he had a little time to see how she'd manage. Coldwater Creek had a regular preacher but he'd gone the month before to visit with family in Texas. He'd be back in a few days. If he was lucky, his soon-to-be wife would have changed her mind about marrying him before the preacher got back.

Of course, that would still leave the problem of what to do about Nora and her plan to marry Lewis Grimsby.

Lewis was a good man with a successful ranch, and since their properties joined at the east boundary, she wouldn't be too far away.

The problem tumbled around in Cooper's mind. If Josie did change her mind about marrying him, that would change Nora's plans. She wouldn't leave them to marry Lewis. She'd sacrifice her own happiness for Drew and Andy and him. He couldn't let her do that.

There was only one solution – marry Josie like he'd offered to do. He didn't have to like it, though. He'd take care of her, and he'd have to be nice enough to her that she didn't change her mind, but other than that, he'd stay away from her as much as he could.

His plan settled in his brain, he picked up another nail and hammered it into the roof.

Josie put the last of her clothes away. Until Nora got married, she'd be sharing her bedroom.

As she took one of her blouses out of her trunk and shook out the wrinkles, a knock came to the door.

"Come in," she called out.

Nora opened the door and came inside. Josie smiled. "This is your room," she said. "You don't have to knock."

"I thought you might want some privacy since I doubt you got much on the journey here."

"That's true," Josie replied with a chuckle, "but I grew up in an orphanage. Eight of us shared one room. Privacy wasn't something any of us had … ever."

"I didn't think of that. It must have been terrible to grow up without being able to have any time alone."

"I suppose it was, but I was used to it."

"Are you hungry? Lunch is almost ready and you can meet Drew and Andy."

Josie was famished, but the thought of facing Cooper again as well as meeting his brother and nephew made her stomach churn. Or was that hunger? Either way, she felt as if she'd be better off heading straight to the outhouse rather than the kitchen table so that she didn't embarrass herself.

"Come on down when you're ready," Nora went on. "We'll wait for you."

"I'm really not hungry," she lied.

Nora took a step toward her. "You're looking positively peaked. You have to eat something. You're nervous, aren't you?"

Josie thought she'd been hiding her trepidation well, but it seemed Nora could see right through it. There was no point in denying it. She nodded. "Your brother offered to marry me," she began.

Nora grinned. "I knew he would. You're so pretty—"

"He's not doing it because he cares about me or how I look," Josie protested. "He's doing it because he knows you won't marry unless he does and he's willing to do whatever he has to so that you will. I'm not sure I can marry a man who doesn't want me."

Nora grabbed Josie's hand. "He will by the time the preacher gets here. I just know it. You just have to get to know him. He'll be a good husband, Josie."

"I'm sure he will—"

"And I'm sure that when he gets to know you, he'll be glad he married you," Nora went on. "It's just a shame there isn't time for you two to fall in love before Lewis and I get married. Lewis is really anxious now that you're here."

"When will the preacher be back?" Josie asked.

"In a few days, I expect. As soon as he's home, I'm going to go and see him to make arrangements to have the wedding as soon as we can. And once you and Cooper are married, we're all going to be happy."

Josie wished she had that much confidence. "I know how to cook and clean and look after children," she said. "I know how to do …" She lowered her voice a little. "… manly chores too, like repair things and build furniture."

"That's wonderful," Nora said. "You'll be such a good ranch wife."

"I don't know anything about men, though," she admitted. "I've never had a suitor."

"I don't know much more, but I think most of it comes naturally. Now, I'm going to set lunch out. Come downstairs when you're ready and meet the rest of the family."

Nora hurried out, closing the door behind her. Josie heard her light footsteps on the stairs as she lifted another blouse out of her trunk.

She felt her brow crease in a frown. What exactly was supposed to come naturally?

our pairs of eyes looked up at Josie as she came into the kitchen. She thought she saw Cooper's eyes narrow slightly, but then he gave her a tiny smile.

"There you are," Nora said, bounding up from her chair beside Cooper and crossing to slide an arm around Josie's shoulders. "Come on in and sit down."

She led Josie to the chair beside Drew and directly opposite Cooper.

Josie sat down, thankful her trembling legs hadn't collapsed.

"It's nice to meet you, Miss Parker," Drew said, once Nora had made the introductions. "I hope you'll be happy here."

"Thank you," she replied, returning the welcoming smile he'd sent her, "and please call me Josie."

It was easy to see the resemblance between Drew and

Cooper. Both had black hair, but while Cooper had deep blue eyes, Drew's were lighter. His face was leaner, too, and his jawline a little less square than Cooper's. Still, he was a handsome man. It seemed good looks ran in the family.

"And this is Andy," Drew added, turning to the little blonde boy kneeling on the chair beside him. "Andy, say hello to Miss Parker."

The boy gazed at her intently, then introduced himself. "How do you do, Miss Parker. My name is Andy Thompson." Then he sent a questioning glance toward Drew. Drew nodded and smiled.

"It's a pleasure to meet you, Andy Thompson," she replied with a grin.

"I hear you and Cooper are tying the knot," Drew said as he stabbed a slice of meat on the platter in the middle of the table and put it on his plate.

Heat flooded Josie's cheeks. She waited for Cooper to comment, but he lowered his head and focused on the food on his plate. "It seems that way," she said finally.

"In fact," Nora burst in, "I've been thinking about this. Why don't you come with me when I go see the preacher? We can have a double wedding. I can't get married until you do, since you can't very well live here with two grown men without the busybodies in town ripping your reputation to shreds."

Still there was no response from Cooper. What was he thinking? Was he filled with regret for offering to marry her? She wished she knew. She'd always been honest – sometimes brutally so – and she preferred that in other people as well, even if the truth was sometimes painful to hear.

If he was sorry for his words earlier, she wanted to know.

Josie found the rest of the meal awkward, but it was apparent the others didn't feel the same. The subject of weddings faded amid talk centered around ranch chores, news from town, and Andy's description of the caterpillar he'd found outside earlier that morning. It now had a new home in a cardboard box filled with grass and dirt.

Josie found Andy's chatter delightful, and she couldn't help but notice the difference between meals at this table and those she'd eaten quietly at the orphanage. Of course, having silence at the table there made sense. The noise of thirty or so children all speaking at once would have been unbearable.

None too soon, Drew excused himself to take Andy with him while they checked on one of the horses who'd cut his leg. A minute or so later, Cooper excused himself and left, too.

"Well, that was pleasant," Nora remarked sarcastically once the men were gone and she and Josie were clearing the table. "Cooper didn't speak directly to you once."

"It was a little uncomfortable," Josie agreed. "I don't know how we can get to know each other when he won't even talk to me."

Nora carried one of the empty pottery bowls to the dry sink. "He'll come around. Why don't you go and talk to him while I take care of the dishes?"

"I don't mind helping you first," Josie said, looking out

the window. Cooper was in the yard, an axe in one hand as he set a log on a stump with the other. Then he stood back, and as she watched, he swung the axe in a high arc. His muscles tensed beneath his shirt, and the axe came down, splitting the wood cleanly as if it were butter. The two smaller pieces of wood fell off the stump and landed in the dirt.

As she watched, he picked them up and tossed them into a pile behind him, then took another log, set it on the stump and repeated the process.

Nora waved away her offer. "It's easier if I do it myself. Besides," she added with a grin, "I'd really like you two to at least be on speaking terms before the wedding."

Josie would like that, too, but by the silence from him at the table, she wondered if he planned to ever talk to her again.

Well, she mused as she crossed the kitchen and opened the door, no time like the present to find out.

Josie stepped outside and closed the door quietly behind her. The pine-scented breeze ruffled her hair, and she paused for a few moments to tuck the stray curls behind her ears.

Cooper looked up as she crossed the yard to where he was chopping wood, then returned to his task.

Josie stopped a few feet away, far enough that there was no risk of being hit by flying wood chips.

"Something I can do for you?" he asked finally.

"I wondered ... that is ... can I help you?"

"Help?" he asked. "Help me what? I'm chopping wood. There isn't anything you can help with."

She glanced around. She hadn't really stopped to think about exactly how she could help him, only that it was an excuse to talk to him. Her gaze stopped at the pile of wood beside him. "Chopping firewood is hard work," she commented, "and since you don't need it until winter I'm surprised you don't wait until fall when it's cooler."

"The wood needs time to dry out or it won't burn."

"Oh." She'd never seen anyone chopping wood before. In Chicago, firewood magically appeared in the shed beside the orphanage in late autumn.

"What will you do with the wood once you've chopped it?"

"I'll stack it in the lean-to and let it dry out in the heat." He jerked his head in the direction of a makeshift roof and two posts attached to the back of the house. A few pieces of firewood lay on the ground beneath it.

"I see."

"I need to get back to work, so if there's nothing else ..." He leaned the axe against the stump and turned away.

Well, Josie thought, surely there's something I can do to help, even if he doesn't think so. Her gaze scanned the yard, and a hint of a smile teased her lips.

Without a word, Josie crossed to the ever-growing pile of wood. Since both the lean-to and the wood pile were behind Cooper, he couldn't see what she was doing. She smiled to herself. He likely thought she'd gone inside.

The wheelbarrow would make the job easier, she

knew, but using one was a skill she'd never been able to master. Crouching, she filled her arms with wood, then took them and arranged them in a row along the length of the lean-to.

She'd stacked three rows of wood before Cooper's voice cut through the silence. "What are you doing?"

Josie frowned. He sounded ... confused, although why he would be was a mystery to her. It was plain to see what she was doing. "I'm stacking the wood," she replied. "Is there a special way you like it done?"

He put the axe down and closed the gap between them. "No, but that's too heavy work for a woman."

She met his eyes squarely. "I'm stronger than I look."

"Well ... still ..."

He was flustered, and Josie couldn't help but grin. "I'll stop if I get too tired," she said.

"I don't expect you to do a man's work as well as your own once we ... once Nora leaves."

Josie couldn't help but notice his reluctance to admit they were getting married. Was this how he was going to feel for the rest of their lives? She might mention it at some point, but right now, it was more important for them to have a conversation.

"I don't like to be idle," she said, "and once we're married and Nora is living in her own home, I may not have much time. If I do, though, I'd like to help you and Drew with the ranch chores as much as I can."

"Suit yourself." He walked away and picked up the axe, returning to his chores.

Josie wasn't ready to go back inside, so she stacked

the wood as he chopped it until he was finished.

Without speaking, he put the axe in the wheelbarrow and took them both into the barn. Josie waited for him until he came back outside.

"Will this be enough wood or will you need to chop more?" she asked.

He studied the neat rows she'd made. "More than enough, I expect."

"I see." In a way, Josie was disappointed.

"You did a good job," he said quietly. "There's enough air circulating that it'll dry right out before winter. Have you done this before?"

She shook her head. "In Chicago, I think someone brought the wood and stacked it. I saw it and how it looked so I assumed that was the right way."

"It is." He smiled at her then, and again she noticed how nice his smile was. She wished he'd smile more often.

She was surprised she really wanted to spend more time with him, to see that smile again and to learn more about him and the farm. "What are you going to do now?" she asked. "Can I help?"

"I think it's best if you go inside now. You don't want to get too sunburned, and already your nose is pink."

Her hand flew to her nose. It definitely felt warmer than it should. "Oh ..."

"It'd be a shame to ruin that pretty skin of yours," he went on.

Heat rose in her cheeks, and she wondered if it was as obvious as it felt.

"I'm going to ride out to the north field and see if Drew needs some help," he went on, " but we'll be back in time for supper."

Josie watched him walk away, heading toward the barn. A smile tugged at her lips. He'd called her pretty ... well, sort of.

And for some reason she didn't understand, she felt as if butterflies were fluttering in her veins. It was a strange sensation, and if she was being completely honest with herself, she liked it.

Josie didn't see Cooper for the rest of the afternoon, and by the time he came inside for supper, Josie's nerves were at the breaking point.

Sitting across from him at the table, Nora prattled on about the preacher's arrival and how everything was going to work out so perfectly for everyone.

Josie wasn't so sure. It would hardly be a perfect life if Cooper avoided her whenever he could, and if he didn't even speak to her when they were forced to be in the same room together.

Cooper sat through the meal without saying a word, his gaze glued to the food on his plate. Finally, everyone had finished eating. Josie bounded up from the table and began gathering the dirty dishes to take to the dry sink.

"You and Cooper need to talk," Nora said, blocking Josie's path to the sink and taking the plates out of her hands. "I'll take care of these."

"It's not necessary—" What she could say to Cooper, she didn't know, and by his silence during the meal, she was pretty sure he didn't have anything to say to her either.

Nora glared at Cooper. "Cooper, take Josie out to the porch. If you two are going to be husband and wife, you need to at least talk to each other."

Josie saw Cooper sigh, but he rose from the table and set his napkin beside his plate. He gave Josie a faint smile. "Guess we'd better do what we're told. One thing I know about my sister, when she sets her mind on getting somebody to do something, she doesn't let up until they give in."

Nora grinned, then turned away toward the sink.

Cooper opened the front door and stepped aside to let Josie go first. Night had fallen and the searing heat of the day had faded. Stars twinkled overhead and the faint scent of pine and cedar floated on a soft breeze.

"I'm not sure what Nora expects us to talk about," Cooper finally said when she was seated in one of the rocking chairs on the porch. She expected him to occupy the other, but instead he leaned his hips against the porch railing, directly in front of her.

Josie let out a short chuckle. "I'm not sure either, but she's right. If we're going to be married, we should at least talk."

"I suppose we should."

What could they talk about? The weather? That would hardly help them get to know each other. Finally, after an awkward silence, she thought of something. "Perhaps you could tell me about your ranch."

His face was cast in the glow from a lantern hanging on a nail nearby and the light streaming through the window from inside, and Josie could see the smile creasing his lips.

"I bought this land four years ago. It's a little less than a thousand acres, but it's plenty for me. I have no need to be rich, so if you're looking for a husband who has enough money to buy you jewels and other frippery, you'd best look somewhere else."

Josie's hackles rose. That he would assume she was a gold-digger infuriated her. "I can assure you I have no need for frippery," she snapped. "I only ask for a roof over my head and food in my stomach, and enough money to provide for any children we might have in the future."

Realizing she'd implied that they'd ... that he'd want to exercise his marital rights one day, her face burned with embarrassment. She began to form an apology in her mind, but then decided against it, hoping he hadn't really heard her.

Her hopes were dashed when he spoke again.

"You wanting a real marriage then?"

Drat! He had heard her! "I ... didn't mean ... that is ..."

He laughed then, the sound rich and deep. Small creases formed at the corners of his eyes. He was pleasant to look at when he was serious, but when he smiled and his eyes twinkled the way they did in the lamplight, he was so handsome it almost took her breath away. In that moment, she made it a goal to do her best to see him smile and laugh more often.

"Don't worry, Josie," he said once his laughter had subsided, "I figured it was a slip of the tongue."

She raised her head to meet his eyes. "It was."

"But it does raise a few questions," he said, straightening and crossing to the rocking chair beside her. He shifted it so that he could see her face without twisting around and lowered himself into it. "Why did you travel all this way to marry a man you didn't know?"

She didn't answer immediately. She was sure that telling her future husband that her decision to marry him seemed like the lesser of two evils wasn't the right way to start a relationship. Yet it was the truth, and Josie believed in being honest, no matter what.

"I didn't see I had a choice," she said quietly. "My friend Sally was in the same situation a while ago. She had to leave the orphanage. She tried to find work, but couldn't."

"So she became a mail-order bride?"

Josie shook her head. "She works in a brothel back in Chicago. I couldn't …"

"I see."

"So you took a chance and came here."

"I did."

"Did you stop to think that I might have been a drunkard, or that I might beat you?"

"I knew that I could be a good wife. I had to gamble

that you were a good man who'd be a good husband. I hope I made the right decision."

Cooper couldn't reassure her. He wasn't sure if he'd be a good husband or not. Hell, he wasn't even sure what a good husband was. He'd never even given marriage much thought. He'd always been content with his life the way it was. He'd never seen any need to add a wife to it.

And going by most of the married women he knew, they were whiny and demanding and criticized their men from sunup to sundown. He sure didn't need that.

He had his ranch. He had his family. He didn't need anything else. If he hadn't had Nora and Drew and Andy, though …

"Did you always live in the orphanage?" he asked.

"Yes," she replied. "As far back as I remember. Mrs. Norton says my parents left me there when I was only a few days old. My papa said they couldn't look after me."

"And there was no other family to help?"

Josie lowered her gaze and shook her head.

"I'm sorry," he said softly. "I can't imagine what it must have been like to grow up without family. Mine has always been there, even when I wished they weren't."

Josie's head jerked up and her eyes widened. "Why would you ever wish that?"

"Oh, don't get me wrong. I love them, but sometimes … it would be nice to not have people think that because they're family, they can run your life, tell you what to eat and when, how to spend your money, what woman to court—"

A giggle escaped from Josie's lips. She clapped her hand over her mouth. "Really? They do that?"

The sound of her laughter warmed his insides, and he couldn't help but smile. "Didn't my sister just find me a wife?"

"Oh ... that's true ... but honestly, I don't think I'd mind knowing I have someone who cares about me enough to worry about what I'm eating or where I'm spending my money—"

"Or who you marry," he put in. "I know her heart was in the right place, but she took things too far this time."

Josie nodded. "She did. And I'm sorry I put you in such a terrible position that you feel obligated to marry me—"

"I don't feel obligated, so don't think that. And you didn't put me in this position. Nora did. Her and her interfering, even though I know she was doing what she thought was best for Andy."

"It must be wonderful to have people love you that much."

"One day, I'll remind you of this conversation, because once we're married, you'll officially be part of the family and eventually, you'll become a victim, too. Hell, I wouldn't be surprised if Nora decides when we should start having babies."

He stopped talking, surprised that he'd revealed so much to a woman he barely knew. He'd often thought it would be nice to be alone, but he'd never voiced it to anybody.

He had to admit that as well as being one of the prettiest women he'd ever seen, Josie was easy to talk to. She hadn't told him he was wrong to feel that way, and she seemed to understand, even though her family had deserted her.

And why had the idea of babies suddenly popped into his head? Must have been Josie's remark earlier, but now that he thought about it, he wouldn't mind a son or two like Andy. Or maybe a daughter like Josie, with her hair the same shade as wheat after a rainfall and her eyes the color of whiskey.

He should get away from her now and stay away from her as much as possible. Something about her was drawing him to her, making him think about things he'd never thought of before. And he didn't like it. He was happy with his life the way it was. Marrying her was a way for Nora to have the life she wanted and for Andy to be taken care of. Nothing more.

In a few days, they'd be married. She'd be his, body and soul, and he'd be within his rights to bed her as often as he wanted to.

A slow heat began building low in his belly as his gaze raked over her, taking in her curves, and lips that seemed ripe for kissing.

He didn't plan to like her much, and he sure as hell wasn't going to fall in love with her, but dammit, he wouldn't mind having her in his bed.

CHAPTER 4

"*P*lease let me do something," Josie said to Nora the morning before the wedding once Cooper and Drew were gone for the day. Nora hadn't let her lift a finger since she arrived, and if she had to sit by and watch Nora do all the work for one more second, she'd scream. She was used to being busy, to doing her part to help at the orphanage. She'd been grateful the first day or two, because she was tired from her trip, but soon the exhaustion had faded and her energy level had returned.

And if she was busy, she wouldn't have time to think about the wedding the next day. Her stomach felt as if it was twisted into a giant knot, and she found herself unable to concentrate on anything without her mind drifting to Cooper—and their future.

Her reaction to Cooper whenever he was near frightened her. When he smiled at her, a strange sensation washed over her, and if his hand happened to graze hers, why her whole being suddenly heated as if she was on fire.

She supposed she could ask Nora if she'd ever had the same reaction to a man, but she couldn't bring herself to speak of such things.

"There's no need to do anything," Nora replied. "I have a routine that I'm used to."

"It'll help me if I start now so that I'm familiar with how things are done. After all, you'll be living at Lewis's farm after tomorrow."

Nora folded a towel and stacked it with the others on the table in the kitchen. "That's why you should rest now," she said. "After the wedding, you'll have plenty to do. It's a beautiful day. Why don't you go and sit on the porch and rest? You must still be exhausted from your journey out here."

"Not at all, and I find it difficult to be idle. I'm not used to it, and I really do want to help."

"Well, if you insist on doing something, you can go out and see if there's enough fruit of any kind that's ripe enough to make a pie for dessert tonight. Are you a good cook?"

"Cooking was one of my tasks at the orphanage and nobody complained," she replied with a laugh.

"Then I'm sure Cooper and Drew won't either. Those men would eat buffalo hide if it was put on a plate in front of them."

Josie took a basket off a shelf and hurried outside, rounding the house and heading toward a large vegetable garden. Nearby, bushes laden down with berries lined a fence.

It didn't take long before she'd filled the basket with enough blackberries and raspberries to bake at least two pies. She popped a raspberry into her mouth, her tongue tingling with the taste of the sweet juice.

As she walked back toward the house, a movement near the barn caught her attention. Two horses were grazing in a fenced corral, one black and the other brown with a white streak down its face and white boots.

Josie had only ever been near one horse, and she couldn't resist moving closer. As she approached the enclosure, the black horse looked up and took a few steps toward her. She reached her hand over the fence, and her heartbeat skittered in her ribs when the horse nudged her hand with its head, but she didn't move away. Instead, she ran her palm down its neck, a smile tugging at her lips.

She stopped, and the horse nudged her again, signaling he liked her touch.

"Do you ride?" The voice coming from behind startled her, and she spun around to face Cooper.

"No," she replied. "I lived in a city. There was no need to ride, and the orphanage only had one horse. We weren't allowed to go near him."

"Then I'll teach you after the wedding. You should know how to ride in case you ever need to get to town without hitching up the wagon. Is this the first time you've been near a horse?"

"Not exactly," she said. "I was near one other horse—once. I didn't touch her, though."

"Why not?"

"She was … it was about two years ago. I was helping Hank, he's the handyman at the orphanage, to fix a broken window in Mr. Kalinack's stable. He had a mare. Her name was Tulip. I was holding the glass when suddenly, the mare dropped down onto the straw. She was panting and grunting. I thought she was dying. Mr. Kalinack told me to go back to the orphanage, that the mare was about to give birth and that it was nothing a female should see."

"Did you?"

Josie grinned. "No. I went outside and climbed on a crate so I could see inside."

"So you make a habit of not doing what you're told?"

For a moment or two, she thought he was angry, but the glint in his eye told her he was teasing.

"Not if there's no good reason to."

"Protecting you from something unpleasant isn't a good enough reason?"

"If I need protecting, I'll say so."

"Fair enough," he said with a laugh. "So you disobeyed and you saw the mare give birth?"

"I did. It was terrifying, but then the baby got up and it was beautiful."

The horse snorted, as if to remind Josie she was still there.

"This is Lola," Cooper said, "and the chestnut is Darby. Lola's going to be a mama soon."

"Really?"

He nodded. "Giving birth can be terrifying to watch, but if you're interested in a closer look, I'll let you know when it's time. You can even help if you've a mind to."

"So you don't think it's inappropriate for a woman?"

He laughed. "I don't think it's something a woman should watch and I'd rather you didn't, but I have a feeling what other people think you should or shouldn't do isn't important to you. And I think that if you somehow found out when Lola was giving birth and you wanted to see it, you'd find a way to peek in and watch anyway. I'd rather let you watch from where it's safe than risk you hurting yourself."

Josie giggled. He must have read her mind.

Was she really lucky enough to have found a man who'd let her do the things she wanted to do even when he didn't fully approve? That she'd be allowed to do what Mrs. Norton always called "man's work"?

Her respect for Cooper inched upward. Not only was he handsome, devoted to his family and his home, but he was a man ahead of his time.

He was an unusual man indeed.

Dusk was falling by the time Cooper and Drew finished tending the horses that evening and crossed the yard to the house.

"Smells good," Drew commented as they stepped inside.

"Smells good," Andy repeated.

The men laughed, and Cooper nodded in agreement as mouth-watering aromas met his nose.

"Supper's just about ready," Nora called out from the kitchen.

"Papa, come play trains with me." Andy took Drew's hand and tugged. Drew followed him into the corner of the main room where two wooden trains sat on the floor.

Cooper strolled through the house to the kitchen where Josie was taking a tray of biscuits out of the oven and Nora was setting the table.

Unaware of him watching them, the two women bustled about as if they'd been working together in the same kitchen for years.

Nora finally noticed him and waved the wooden spoon in her hand. "Either come in and sit down or go out, but do one or the other instead of standing there getting in the way."

Where he was leaning against the wall in the doorway with his ankles crossed and his arms folded across his chest, he wasn't in anybody's way, but it was best not to argue with Nora whenever he could avoid it. He thought about going back into the main room and joining Drew and Andy in their game, but he found himself more interested in looking at Josie. He wandered into the kitchen and slid into a chair at the table.

Josie's face was flushed with the heat from the oven and her hair had come loose from the knot at the back of her neck, but somehow it only made her prettier.

She reached for a bowl from the shelf above the dry sink and her curves strained at the fabric of her blouse. A slow heat wormed its way through him and settled low in his belly.

As if she sensed him watching her, Josie turned to face him and sent him a shy smile as she set a bowl of chicken and dumplings on the table. Nora added a plate of biscuits and a bowl of butter.

Nora moved to the doorway and called to Drew and Andy to come to the table.

"Josie made supper tonight," Nora informed him once they were all seated at the table and Cooper had said the blessing.

That explained Josie's sudden silence. He'd gotten the impression earlier that she liked to talk, yet she hadn't said a word since he'd come into the house.

He glanced over at her, her head still lowered. She looked … scared. Was she worried he wouldn't like the meal? Hell, even if he didn't, he'd choke it down if only the worry he saw on her face would disappear.

Andy made a face when Drew spooned some food onto his plate. "I don't like that."

Josie's eyes widened. "I'm sorry … I didn't know …"

Drew smiled at her. "Don't worry. He likes it. He's just being ornery because he's tired." Then, turning to his son, he said quietly, "It's not polite to not eat when someone takes the time to make you supper."

"I don't like it," he repeated. "I want pie."

"Pie?" Drew sent a questioning look in Josie's direction.

"I made pies for dessert," she told him. "Andy saw them cooling on the windowsill."

Drew nodded his understanding and turned back to Andy. "No pie until you finish your supper," he said softly.

"I want pie now."

Josie noticed Drew's sigh of exasperation. "Eat your supper."

Andy cocked his head and squinted at Josie. "Can I have pie now?"

"After supper," Josie said. She hoped Drew wouldn't mind her getting involved, but she'd dealt with this kind of situation many times over the years with the smaller children at the orphanage. Not that they'd had pie often, but there had always been children who wanted dessert first. Andy was still young enough that her plan should work. "I even have a magic piece with your name on it, but if you don't hurry and eat your supper, your name will disappear and then anyone can eat it."

Cooper hid a grin behind his napkin and for a few moments, no one spoke. Josie turned back to her meal and spooned the chicken and dumplings onto her plate. Then, out of the corner of her eye, she saw Andy pick up his spoon and shovel a piece of dumpling soaked in gravy into his mouth.

Drew smiled at Josie and mouthed a "thank you" in her direction. "Nora, I think Josie's going to do just fine here, don't you?"

Josie blushed at the compliment. She did know how to deal with children. Now if only she could find a way to make Cooper like her ... preferably before the wedding ... she'd be a happy woman.

Since it was bad luck for the groom to see the bride before the wedding, right after supper Nora shuffled Cooper off with Drew and Andy to spend the night.

As soon as they were gone, Nora hurried up the stairs. "Come on, let's get started," she announced.

Josie was confused. "Get started on what?" she asked, following. She stopped behind Nora when she opened her bedroom door and went inside.

"Moving your things into Cooper's room."

Josie's eyes widened and a flush of embarrassment swept through her. "Oh ... no ... we can't ..."

"Of course we can," Nora insisted. "You're going to be married tomorrow. Don't tell me you planned to still sleep in here."

"I'm sure Cooper won't approve."

Nora waved away her objections, opened the wardrobe and took out the hangers holding Josie's clothes. She draped them over her arm and brushed past her, heading to Cooper's room.

"Please don't—"

Nora turned back to face her. "How can you ever have a real marriage if you don't even share a bedroom?"

"We aren't ... I mean, this isn't a real marriage ..."

"And it won't be unless you start out acting as if it is. And I know my brother. Once he gets used to the idea, he'll be happy to have a wife." She wiggled her eyebrows and grinned. "And be sharing a bed. So you should sleep in there tonight to get used to it."

"He's going to be so angry ..." Josie murmured, more to herself than to Nora. It was obvious Nora wasn't going to listen, so there was no point in trying to make her change her mind. Maybe as soon as they got back from the church, she could move her things back into the other room before he knew what his sister had done.

Still, she'd have to spend one night in his bed, so she postponed it as long as she could. Finally, she felt her eyes drifting closed and she had to retire.

It felt so strange to walk into Cooper's bedroom and close the door. His room was the same size as Nora's, but where hers was more feminine, Cooper's furniture was heavy and solid. Heavy maroon curtains hung at the window and a quilt of maroon, blue and hunter green covered the bed.

Josie undressed and climbed into bed. His scent lingered on the pillows beneath her head and she couldn't help wondering which side of the bed he slept on, if he had any preference at all.

Nora's words came back to her. Act as if they had a real marriage. Could she do that?

She knew what sharing a bed with Cooper would mean. Could it really be as horrible as Sally had described? She couldn't imagine Cooper hurting her or doing the things to her Sally had mentioned.

Josie did want children of her own one day. She'd always enjoying taking care of the babies and young children in the orphanage, and already she'd come to love Andy. She couldn't imagine loving her own children more, but she'd heard that there was no other love like it.

She wanted to experience that for herself, and there was only one way to do it. She'd have to allow Cooper to kiss her, and touch her, and ... whatever else he chose to do.

What would his lips feel like against hers? What would his hands feel like on her body? The questions rolled around in her mind, and at the same time, a strange warmth built inside her. A sense of anticipation washed over her and she realized that the thought of being with Cooper wasn't entirely unpleasant. No, she decided, Cooper would never treat her the way men treated Sally. She was sure of it.

She was still thinking about him when she dozed off to sleep.

It seemed to be only moments later when the raucous crowing of the rooster woke her.

Josie stared at the ceiling as the first rays of morning filtered through a gap in the heavy curtains on the window. Her stomach twisted, her throat was dry, and her heart felt as if it was going to explode.

She threw off the thin coverlet, the floor cold under her feet. She padded across the room to the window and gazed outside. It had rained the night before, but now, the sun slowly rose on the horizon, casting a pinkish-gold glow on the fields. She smiled. It looked as if the sun was going to shine for her wedding.

Her wedding!

CHAPTER 5

*A*ndy licked a dollop of jam off his finger. "You getting married too, Papa?"

Drew and Cooper exchanged glances. "No," Drew answered.

"Why not?"

Cooper drained his coffee and leaned back in his chair, wondering how Drew was going to answer his son's question. "Because I don't have a lady to marry."

"Why not?"

"Because ..."

"Do we got to go to church soon?"

Cooper saw Drew's sigh of relief when Andy's questions strayed from his father's marriage plans, and grinned.

"We do. Now if you're finished your breakfast, go upstairs and get dressed."

"You got to help me."

"I'll be up in a minute," Drew said.

Andy climbed down and raced out of the room.

"The boy has a good point," Cooper commented once he could hear Andy's footsteps on the floor above his head. "You should be getting married instead of me."

Drew stirred the strong black brew in his mug. "Don't think I don't appreciate what you're doing for me and Andy," he said. "I do. And you're right. I should be getting married again so that Andy has a ma. It wasn't your responsibility to make sure there was a woman here to take care of him."

"So why am I the one marrying Josie and not you? She doesn't care who she marries." Even as he said the words, a knot formed in his stomach and his lungs seemed to refuse to expand enough for him to take a deep breath.

He'd told the truth. She'd come to Montana to marry a stranger, so it wouldn't have mattered to her whether she married him or Drew.

But it mattered to him. He didn't know why, but the thought of her being with another man … letting another man bed her …

"You okay?" Drew's voice held concern. "What's the matter? Getting cold feet?"

Cooper looked at his brother and shook his head. "No. Just wanting to get it over with, that's all."

Drew stood, picked up his coffee mug and dropped it into the basin of soapy water. Turning to Cooper, he held out his hand. "I hope you'll be as happy as Leta and I were," he said, his voice breaking.

Cooper nodded. "I'll do my best, and I hope one day you'll find another woman you love as much as you loved her."

The aroma of coffee brewing filled Josie's nose as she entered the kitchen. Nora was sitting at the kitchen table, the needle in her hand furiously stitching the mound of cream fabric in front of her.

"What are you doing?" Josie asked.

"Finishing my wedding dress," Nora answered. "I forgot to sew on the lace trim along the hem."

Josie grazed the fabric with the tips of her fingers. It was so soft … so luxurious … "It's lovely," she said softly. She'd likely never have a dress like that, she thought. Not that it would be practical even if she could afford it. Still, she was sure it would feel wonderful against her skin, and it would be nice to buy something just once because she wanted it rather than needed it.

She crossed to the shelf above the dry sink and took down two mugs. "Coffee?" she called over her shoulder.

"Yes, please," Nora replied, "but leave it there. My hands are so shaky I don't want to risk spilling it on my dress."

Josie poured the coffee and took a sip. "You'll be beautiful," she commented, her eyes following Nora's movements.

"I hope Lewis thinks so."

Josie smiled. She'd seen the way Lewis looked at

Nora, as if she was the sun, the moon and the stars all rolled into one. "He will."

Nora slid the thread between her teeth and broke it, then stabbed the needle into the bobbin. "There. Done." She bounded up and scooped the dress up in her arms. "I'll just go and hang this up and be right back. We'd better have some breakfast before we leave for the church."

While Nora was upstairs, Josie sliced a few pieces of bacon and put them in the skillet on the stove. She was cracking eggs into a bowl when Nora got back.

"It just occurred to me, I didn't see your wedding dress when we moved your things into Cooper's room last night," she commented, taking a loaf of bread out of the breadbox.

"I ... I don't really have one," she murmured. She'd worn the best dress she owned the day she arrived in Coldwater Creek. It was hardly suitable for a wedding, but she had no other choice. "It doesn't matter. It's not as if Cooper and I are marrying for love."

"Of course it matters. You need a pretty dress to get married in—" Suddenly, she clapped her hand over her mouth and her cheeks flushed. "Oh, I'm so sorry ... I didn't mean you won't be pretty ... you will ..."

Josie smiled. She understood what Nora had been trying to say. And she was right. It wasn't a wedding dress. "No need to apologize. You're right. It isn't the kind of dress I imagined wearing to my wedding."

Nora wrapped a towel around her hand. She lifted the

skillet off the stove and set it on the counter, then grabbed Josie's hands. "Come with me."

Josie had no choice but to let Nora drag her by the hand through the parlor and up the stairs to Nora's bedroom.

Nora opened the wardrobe and drew out a hanger holding a kingfisher-blue gown with a scooped neckline and puffed sleeves, the whole dress dotted with white flowers. The hem of the skirt was scalloped with white ribbons and showed a white frilly under-petticoat. "It's not really a wedding gown," she said, "but with your coloring, I know you'll look beautiful in it."

Nora handed the gown to Josie. Josie didn't know what kind of fabric it was, but it was expensive, she was sure. She'd never even held such an exquisite gown. "Oh, I couldn't …"

"Of course you can," Nora insisted. "It'll be perfect. In fact, I might not want to get married beside you. You're going to outshine me by a mile."

Josie wasn't used to compliments, and she found herself blushing under Nora's scrutiny.

"Now let's go and get breakfast," Nora said. "We still have to pick some flowers to carry and get dressed. We don't want to be late getting to the church."

Two hours later, Josie stood in front of the mirror in Nora's bedroom. She was stunned by her reflection. The dress hugged her curves as if it had been made especially for her. Nora had styled her hair, piling it on her head with a few strands left loose to frame her face.

Nora stood back and clasped her hands. "Oh, my

goodness, Cooper might not love you now, but one look at you in that gown and he'll be head over heels."

Josie's eyes misted. Nora was right. Even though it was arrogant to think that way about herself, she had to admit she'd never looked or felt more beautiful.

Would Cooper think so? She suddenly realized his reaction was important to her, although she couldn't say why.

Cooper stood at one side of the altar in the front of the church. He hooked his index finger into the collar of his Sunday shirt and tugged, trying to loosen it. Right now, it felt as tight as a hangman's noose. Drew stood beside him, while Andy sat in the front pew beside the preacher's sister.

On the other side of the altar, Lewis and his brother waited for Nora.

The doors at the back of the church opened, and Josie and Nora walked in.

Cooper's breath caught in his throat. While his chest tightened at the thought that his sister would now belong to another man, a strange sensation washed over him when his gaze rested on Josie and she raised her eyes to meet his. The world seemed to fade until only Josie filled his vision.

Drew nudged him and whispered something in his ear before he walked down the aisle to meet the two women. He stood between them and smiled at Josie, leaning closer to say something to her. She nodded, and while Cooper looked on, he tucked Josie's hand into one of his elbows and Nora's into the other.

Cooper's breath stuck in his throat. Josie seemed to float toward him and take his outstretched hand.

A few minutes later, the preacher began to speak. Cooper couldn't do anything but stare at Josie standing beside him. He must have answered the preacher's questions, but he couldn't remember one word when it was over and they were pronounced husband and wife.

"Are you going to kiss your bride or not?" the preacher asked. Startled, he looked at the preacher, who was grinning. "Nora and Lewis have already sealed their vows with a kiss. Everybody's waiting for you."

"Oh ... uh ... right ..."

Josie was looking up at him, her face flushed. Was she embarrassed? Did she think he didn't want to kiss her? Hell, he'd thought of little else for the past few days. Now, he had to concentrate on not kissing her the way he'd dreamed of when he finally managed to sleep at night.

He glanced around at the full church, their faces smiling, waiting for him to kiss Josie. He should give them a show and kiss her soundly, he thought, but one look at the expression on her face changed his mind. She looked as if she was facing a firing squad.

Was the woman who'd traveled hundreds of miles to marry a stranger scared of a little kiss?

He wasn't sure, but just in case, he slowly lowered his head toward hers. Her lilac scent wafted toward him as he barely brushed her lips with his. Fire swept through him and it took every ounce of self-control he could muster to stop himself from wrapping his arms around her and never letting her go.

He heard her suck in a breath as he pulled away to a round of applause.

And it was over. He was now a married man, whether he liked it or not.

The wedding feast was in full swing. Josie had been introduced to what seemed like every person in town. She'd never remember any of their names, and she hoped she wouldn't be expected to, at least for a few years. It would likely take that long.

Josie sat at a table near the back corner of the wooden building that housed the school and the town meeting hall. A full plate of food prepared by the ladies in town sat on the table in front of her, but her stomach wouldn't allow her to even try to eat anything.

Cooper was standing with a group of men near a table holding several jugs of lemonade and a bowl of punch. She watched him, still shocked that they were truly married. Wearing the suit she assumed he wore to church on Sundays, the snowy-white shirt contrasted against his sun-bronzed skin. He'd slicked down his black hair for the wedding, but the cowlick she'd noticed whenever he took off his hat wouldn't be tamed. Nora always teased him about it. Josie thought it was adorable.

As she looked on, Lewis joined the group of men. A second or two later, Nora dropped into the chair beside her. "Lewis and I are going to leave now," she said.

Josie smiled at her new sister-in-law. "I expect Cooper will want to get back to the ranch soon, too."

Nora reached over and took Josie's hand. "I want to tell you how much I appreciate what you've done for me," she began. "I should never have done what I did and I only hope you and Cooper can find some happiness together."

"I hope so, too," Josie said quietly. She gave Nora a tiny smile. "I truly believe life turns out the way it's meant to, so the way I got here might not have been ideal, but I believe I was meant to come here. Time will tell me why."

She glanced up and saw Lewis crossing the room toward the table. "Your husband is looking for you. I wish you nothing but the best."

The two women got up and hugged each other, and then Lewis led Nora away.

Josie had barely sat back down when Cooper approached. "We should be getting back to the ranch, too," he said. "It's getting late."

Josie got back to her feet and nodded. "Will Drew and Andy be coming with us?"

"No. They're going to stay for a while. Drew offered to take care of the chores tonight so we can have some time alone."

Josie's throat tightened and her heart skipped a beat.

She'd assumed Drew and Andy would spend the evening with them as they often did.

Instead, she'd be alone with Cooper.

Totally, completely alone!

The house was so quiet! Cooper was in the barn and Josie was by herself for the first time since she arrived in Coldwater Creek. Actually, she couldn't remember really being alone … ever, other than the few minutes every day when she took care of personal needs.

In the orphanage, there were always so many people around, and even on her journey to Colorado, she was surrounded by other travelers.

Something else she'd have to get used to.

She didn't have time to think about that now though, she mused. She'd have to be quick if she expected to get all her things back into Nora's room before Cooper came back in.

Taking off the delicate shawl she'd borrowed from Nora, she folded it and hurried up the stairs to put it on the bureau in Nora's room. She chuckled to herself. For once, she was glad she didn't own much. It wouldn't take too long to move everything back.

She was half done when she turned from the wardrobe to find Cooper standing in the doorway. She'd heard the front door close but she hadn't heard his footsteps on the stairs. She'd hoped she'd be finished before he came up.

"What are you doing?" he asked, his gaze settling on the pile of clothes in her arms.

Her cheeks burned with embarrassment.

"Nora thought we should … that is, I should—"

"Move in?" He smiled.

"Yes," she said. "I disagreed, but when your sister gets a notion in her head …"

He laughed then, the deep sound filling the room. "You don't have to tell me about Nora."

"Of course. I'm sorry," she said.

"Where were you going with the clothes?"

"I was taking them back to Nora's room."

"Why?"

She didn't answer for a few seconds, searching for the right words. She might as well be honest and clear the air, she decided. Raising her head, she met his gaze squarely. "I'm sure you'd rather have your room to yourself, and since Nora's room is empty now, there's no reason why I shouldn't sleep there."

"There is one reason," he said quietly.

He didn't have to say the words. Josie knew exactly what he was referring to. Her heartbeat skittered in her chest and her body flooded with warmth.

His kiss after the preacher pronounced them husband and wife, brief that it was, had rocked her to her core. Never in her life had she been so aware of every nerve ending in her body, every sensation.

She'd wanted the kiss to go on forever. And she'd wanted more than a kiss. She'd wanted his arms around her, wanted to feel his touch.

That desire had blended with guilt that she was having such impure thoughts in God's house.

She felt the same way now, minus the guilt. She smiled as he took a step toward her. "Do you want me to stay?"

"I wouldn't mind," he replied. "Do you want to stay?"

Her breathing grew shallow, and her entire body began to tremble. Whether from fear or excitement, she couldn't say, and if she was being honest, she didn't really care. "I wouldn't mind."

His eyes darkened and his voice deepened. "You know what I'm asking?"

She did know, but she didn't answer immediately. She had no experience with men at all other than the delivery man who used to wink at her when he brought fresh vegetables into the kitchen at the orphanage.

How could she possibly please a man like Cooper? She couldn't, and he'd be sorry he'd married her, and they'd start their life together with him resenting her.

He moved away. "I understand."

So many thoughts had gone through her mind that she'd taken too long to respond and now he thought she didn't want a real marriage.

She reached out and wrapped her fingers around his muscled forearm. "No," she said, "it's not that. I do know what you're asking," she said. "I know what happens, sort of, and that it's horrible for a woman—"

"Who told you it's horrible?" he asked.

"Sally didn't say that exactly, but how can it be anything but horrible?"

He laughed then, and Josie felt her ire stirring. "There's no reason to laugh at me."

"I'm sorry," he said softly. "Trust me, Josie, it's not horrible. Not with the right person. Your friend ... what she does is different ... between two people who care about each other, it's ... good. Very good."

Josie considered that for a few seconds. If he was telling the truth, that would explain why she wanted to feel his lips on hers, feel his hands on her skin. "I don't know what I'm supposed to do. I've never even been kissed before today."

"You've never had a suitor?"

She shook her head. "The only man I've ever spoken to for more than a few minutes is Hank."

"Is that all that's bothering you?"

Now that he'd eased her fears, she could admit that was all she was concerned about. "I don't want to disappoint you."

"You won't," he said. "You definitely won't."

Her nerve endings tingled as he closed the gap between them, his eyes locked on hers. He took the dresses out of her arms and tossed them on a chair in the corner of the room. Then his arms enfolded her and drew her against his hard chest as his head lowered to hers.

Her breath caught in her throat when his lips touched hers and moved against hers, softly and slowly at first. His kiss deepened. One hand splayed across her back, the other moved to sink his fingers into her hair.

Her body turned to liquid and she could feel his heart

beating against her chest. Or was it the sound of her heated blood rushing through her veins?

Heat engulfed her from the top of her head to the tips of her toes, and a heavy sensation settled low in her stomach.

She clutched at his shirt as his tongue pressed against the seam of her lips, urging her to open her mouth. As soon as she did, his tongue plunged inside, tangling with hers in an intimate dance.

She wanted more. Needed more.

She heard him groan, and he gripped her shoulders as he released her mouth. Her lips felt swollen and her breath came in heavy gasps.

His eyes were heavy, his voice gruff. "Are you sure, Josie? Really sure?"

She nodded, her eyes closing as waves of sensation washed over her. "Yes. Oh, yes."

Drawing her close again, he held her tenderly against his chest as he turned down the lamp.

CHAPTER 6

*J*osie woke as dawn was breaking the next morning. She lay in the dim light, listening to Cooper breathing for a few seconds before she turned on her side to look at him.

What she'd experienced the night before in his arms was earth-shattering, nothing at all like what Sally had described.

Not only had Josie felt things she'd never even imagined, she'd acted in ways she never would have thought she was capable of.

And now, in the semi-darkness, she wished she had the nerve to wake Cooper so they could do it again.

As if he sensed he was being watched, his eyes opened and he smiled. "Good morning," he said, his voice hoarse. "How do you feel?"

"Fine," she replied.

He raised himself up and kissed her lightly. "I'm glad.

I was worried. The first time isn't always good for a woman."

She was a little tender, now that he mentioned it. Her face warmed, and she was glad he couldn't see her embarrassment at the turn of the conversation.

She didn't have to worry.

The rooster crowing outside the window drew his attention away from her. He rolled over and got up, reaching for his pants. "I'll go get started on the chores," he said. "Can you handle breakfast?"

"Of course," she replied.

Quickly, she climbed out of bed and pulled on a pale blue work dress. She only had two summer dresses besides the one she'd worn for the trip west. Her only other work dress was almost worn through from washing so much.

She'd never enjoyed sewing so she hadn't practiced much. It looked like she should have since she'd need to sew herself at least one more dress before winter.

Bacon was already sizzling in the skillet on the stove and she was cracking eggs into a bowl when the front door opened. Moments later, she heard Andy's footsteps racing through the house toward the kitchen.

"Good morning, Andy," she said.

A frown furrowed his forehead. "Where's Auntie Nora?"

"She's at Mr. Grimsby's ranch. She's going to live there now."

"Why?"

"They got married yesterday, remember?"

Drew appeared in the kitchen doorway. "I've told him three times already," he said with a laugh. "Andy doesn't like change."

"There are a lot of people who don't like change," she murmured.

Turning her attention back to Andy, she crouched to meet him at eye level. "I'm going to look after you now when your papa and Uncle Cooper are out working."

"I don't want you to." Andy's face scrunched into a scowl. "I want Auntie Nora."

Josie didn't know how to respond. She couldn't show up at Lewis's door the first day and ask Nora to come back to look after Andy.

There had been youngsters at the orphanage who'd had trouble adjusting, but she'd never had to deal with them. She had no idea how.

"Andy, don't be rude." Drew's voice was stern, and he gave Nora a wry smile. "I'm sorry," he mouthed. "I don't know what's gotten into him."

Andy glared at his father and ran out of the room.

As Josie put the scrambled eggs and bacon on the table a few minutes later, she could see Andy sitting in the corner of the parlor, his knees drawn up to his chest, his head down.

It was obvious he was upset and he missed his aunt, but she didn't know how to comfort him, or even if she should.

Drew glanced over at his son but ignored him. "He'll come around," he said to Josie. "He barely remembers his mother already, so he's used to Nora. It'll just take a little time. I'm real sorry I have to leave you to deal with him today, but we have to get that fence fixed out in the north pasture."

Cooper nodded. "Will you be okay with him by yourself?"

"It'll be fine," Josie replied. "I'll have to deal with him alone eventually. Might as well get it over with."

As the door closed behind Cooper and Drew a few minutes later, she frowned at Andy still sitting in the corner.

This was going to be a very long day.

By the time Cooper and Drew loaded up the extra fence posts and tools into the wagon and made their way back to the farmhouse that evening, Cooper was exhausted.

It had been hotter than Hades out in the fields, and he was sure he'd lost ten pounds in sweat. All he wanted now was a tall glass of cold lemonade, some supper, and sleep.

A flash of blue on the front porch caught his attention as he crested the hill leading to the house.

"Looks like Josie managed with Andy," Drew commented once they got close enough to see that both Josie and Andy were sitting on the porch floor facing each other.

As Cooper drew the wagon to a stop in front of the house, Andy scrambled to his feet and raced down the stairs toward Drew. Drew scooped him up and swung him in the air, Andy's squeals of delight piercing the air.

Cooper climbed down out of the wagon and went up the stairs. Josie looked up at him and gave him a shy smile. Her face was flushed from the heat and her dress clung to her curves. Strands of her hair had escaped the tight bun she'd started out with that morning and hung in limp strands. Still, her eyes sparkled and for the first time, he noticed a tiny dimple near the corner of her mouth. He had a sudden urge to kiss it, an urge he tamped down.

"Looks like you and Andy worked things out," he commented.

Josie grinned. "It took an hour or so, but eventually he figured out I'm not the enemy."

"Playing games helped, I expect."

She nodded. "He loves Tiddledywinks."

He looked down at the brightly colored wooden discs on the floor. "Where did they come from?"

She picked up the wooden cup and began putting the discs into it. "I brought it from Chicago," she told him with a short laugh. "It seems silly now, but it was a Christmas gift when I was a child and I've always kept it. I always thought I'd play it with my own children one day."

Cooper's gaze slid over her. Was it possible she was already in the family way? A strange warmth filled him at the thought of a little girl with her wheat-colored hair— and that dimple. Or a son like Andy. For the first time in his life, the thought of having a family of his own wasn't a sour one.

He didn't have to love his children's mother to be a good father. He could provide for her and treat her kindly, but love ... that was not going to happen. That's when the arguments began. He refused to live that way.

"Are you ready for supper?" Josie's voice filtered through his thoughts. "It's ready whenever you are."

"I'll be in as soon as I can," he said, turning away and climbing back into the wagon.

As he unharnessed the horse from the wagon and settled her for the night, he found himself hurrying through his chores.

"It's the strangest thing, Moonbeam," he said to the horse as he filled a pail of oats in her stall. "I missed her today, and I looked forward to coming home."

Supper should be like this every night, Josie thought, her gaze drifting to take in those at the table. Conversation, laughter ... yes, she'd do her best to make supper as pleasant as she could every day.

"I'm thinking about taking Andy to see Leta's parents for a few days," Drew said while Josie was clearing the dinner plates. "That'll give you two some time to really get acquainted—"

Josie and Cooper spoke in unison.

"That's not necessary—"

"You don't have to do that—"

"When Leta was …" Drew looked away for a moment before he faced them again. "When we first got married, we lived alone. It was a good thing, helped us to get used to each other. You both need that. Besides, Andy's grandparents haven't seen him since we moved here, so it's time we went for a visit. If you can handle everything here, that is."

Cooper nodded. "No problem. When are you planning on going?"

"I was thinking about going the day after tomorrow."

Josie brought a dish of cherry crumble to the table.

"Smells good," Cooper said as she spooned it into four bowls.

Josie hoped it tasted as good as it looked. "If you have time one day when Drew gets back, I would like to go into town and stock up on a few things."

"There's nothing pressing tomorrow, is there?" Cooper asked, sending a questioning glance in Drew's direction.

Drew swallowed a mouthful of crumble and shook his head.

"I'll take you tomorrow then, if you like. That way you don't have to wait until Drew gets back," Cooper said to Josie. "Do you have a list?"

Josie shook her head. "I'll make one after I clear from supper. Would it be all right …?" She wasn't sure how much money they had, so she was hesitant to ask for anything.

"What is it, Josie?"

"I wondered … I'd like to buy some fabric for a new work dress, a thin one. In this weather—"

He took a close look at her dress. Josie blushed under his scrutiny. He seemed to be staring at her far longer than necessary.

"You're right," he said finally. "Buy enough fabric for two or three if you like. We don't want you swooning from being overheated."

"Thank you," she said softly, then continued to dish out a bowl for herself.

"You're a good cook, Josie," Cooper commented a few minutes later, pushing his empty dessert bowl away and leaning back in his chair. "Don't ever tell Nora I said it, but that crumble is even better than hers."

Josie blushed. She'd been cooking practically her whole life but she'd always been restricted to *what* she cooked. She loved the thought of being able to cook whatever she wanted for her family.

Her family. She still found it hard to believe she was part of a family, and a wife, even if Cooper didn't really want her.

She didn't love him—at least she didn't think she did—but she was finding she liked him more and more every day. She respected him, and if that was all she'd ever have, it was enough.

Dark clouds scudded across the sky the next afternoon on the way back from town. "Do you think we'll get home before it starts raining?" Josie asked Cooper.

A raindrop splattered on Josie's nose. Cooper reached up and wiped it off with his finger. "I think you have your answer," he said with a smile.

Another drop. And another. Soon, they were both drenched. Luckily, their supplies in the bed of the wagon were covered with canvas.

"Should we find shelter somewhere?" she asked. She'd never noticed any other cabins or anywhere that would provide protection from the weather, but she wasn't as familiar with the surroundings as Cooper was.

He shook his head. "We're wet now. We might as well keep going."

The hardened dirt trail became a river of mud, so it took much longer to reach the ranch than usual. Finally, though, Cooper drew on the reins in front of the house and jumped down. Drew appeared on the porch and between the two men, they quickly got the supplies into the house.

"If you don't need me for anything else right now, Andy needs a nap," Drew said. "We'll be back in time for supper."

"I'll be a little late getting started," Josie told him, "but it should be ready by six."

Josie was in the midst of undressing a few minutes later when Cooper walked into the bedroom. "Oh ..." she cried out, her face burning with embarrassment.

He crossed the room toward her, unbuttoning his wet

shirt and peeling it off. He tossed it on the floor on top of her discarded dress. "You're pretty when your cheeks are flushed," he said.

She braved a quick look at him. Desire shone in his eyes, and a strange kind of warmth stole over her. He closed the gap and kissed her gently.

"I could get used to this," Cooper said a while later, tucking her hair behind her ear and nuzzling her neck.

Josie's voice deserted her, but if she could speak, she would have told him she could get used to it, too. It had only been one day she'd been the mistress of her own home, but she already knew she loved every minute of it. She'd be happy taking care of Cooper, Drew and Andy for the rest of her life.

She hoped Cooper felt the same way.

Cooper's stomach rumbled as he drove the wagon over the crest of a hill toward the ranch house a few afternoons later. Drew and Andy were still away, so he'd hurried through his chores, eager to get back to the house to see Josie. He was finding he missed her during the day when he was out working, and looked forward to seeing her welcoming smile and gentle ways when he came home.

The fact that he liked spending time with her bothered him. He didn't want to like her too much, but she was making it really hard not to. She worked from dusk until dawn in the house, and in the evenings, she mended clothes or sewed by lamplight until she went to bed.

And she never complained about being tired … or too tired for him.

He liked her, and if he wasn't careful, he might even grow to love her.

He wouldn't let that happen. He couldn't let someone else have control over his happiness.

As he neared the house, he thought he heard the sound of hammering coming from inside. It couldn't be, could it? But if not, what was going on?

He drew on the reins in front of the house and climbed down. Suddenly, there was a loud crash from inside the house His heartbeat thumped. *What the—?*

He raced up the stairs and threw open the door. His eyes widened when he saw Josie sitting cross-legged on the floor, her skirt above her knees, her legs and feet bare. She had a hammer in her hand and her lips were pressed together around a nail. An upturned chair lay on the floor in front of her.

She looked up and took the nail out of her mouth as he rushed inside. "What happened? Are you all right?"

She smiled. "I'm fine," she replied. "I'm fixing this chair. It's been wobbly since I got here and one of these days, it's going to break completely if it isn't fixed."

"What was the crash I heard?"

"The chair fell over, that's all."

Relief filled him. "You don't need to be doing repairs," he said, crossing the room and holding out his hand to take the hammer. "That's a man's job. I'll do it for you."

Her brows lifted. "A man's job?"

"That's right."

"I know how to fix a wobbly chair," she pointed out. "I can do it myself. You have enough work to do outside the house."

"I don't mind—"

"Neither do I. If there's a repair I can't handle, you're more than welcome to take care of it, but if it's something simple like this, I'll do it. I miss doing this kind of work. I used to help Hank with something almost every day."

She glared at him. When she spoke again, he could hear the controlled anger in her voice. "Unless you have some objection that makes sense, that is."

He didn't answer immediately. He couldn't think of any reason why she couldn't do what she wanted to do, other than the fact she was a woman. And that wasn't really a reason at all. Finally, he shrugged. "Suit yourself."

She smiled. "Good. I'm glad that's settled." She laid the hammer on the floor and got to her feet, smoothing down her skirt as she did. Cooper had to admit the sight of her long, shapely bare legs had made him forget about food and start thinking about something else.

"Now go and wash up," she said, shooing him out of the kitchen. "I cooked supper early so I'd have time to fix the chair, so it's ready whenever you are."

Cooper nodded and went back outside to wash his hands in the basin Josie always set out for him. As he lathered up the soap and scrubbed his hands, he couldn't help thinking about the woman he'd married. Women cooked and cleaned and had babies. They didn't do repairs. They didn't stack logs. They didn't do many of the chores Josie had done since she'd arrived.

And when he'd heard the crash ... For that few seconds until he'd seen Josie, alive and well, on the floor, he'd been scared. Scared that she'd been hurt ... or worse.

He swore. He didn't want to care that much. Didn't want to find himself worrying about her the way he'd always worried about Nora and Drew and Andy.

But it looked like he had no choice in the matter. Now there was one more person in his life he'd worry about until his dying day.

CHAPTER 7

"*I*t's such a beautiful day, I'd like to go and see Nora this afternoon," Josie said as she and Cooper were finishing breakfast the next day. She wriggled a little in her chair, satisfied that since she'd finished fixing the chair after supper the night before, now she didn't have to worry about it collapsing and her landing on her backside. "May I use the wagon?"

Cooper drained his coffee and set his mug back on the table. "Sorry, but that's not possible. One of the wheels broke so it's in town getting fixed."

Josie was disappointed, but she understood. "It's fine. I'll go another time," she said, trying to force brightness into her voice to offset the disappointment she felt. She hadn't seen Nora since the wedding, and she missed having companionship.

Not that she minded spending time with Cooper, she amended. She was growing fonder of him with every passing day. He had his faults, to be sure. He was untidy sometimes and it never occurred to him to wipe his feet before he dragged dirt into the house. But if that was the worst she had to complain about, she thought with a half-smile, she was a lucky woman.

"So what will you do today then?" Cooper's voice filtered through her thoughts.

She shrugged. "Same as every other day, I expect."

He gazed at her for what seemed a long time, then got up and left the room. When he came back a few minutes later, she was drying their dishes and putting them back on the shelf. She turned when he came in, a frown forming when she saw the pair of pants draped across his arm.

"Here," he said. "Put these on."

"What? Why?"

"It's time you learn to ride, and today's as good a time as any. If I'd taught you like I promised to, you could have taken one of the horses and gone to visit Nora today."

"I can go another time. It's really not important—"

"It is important that you know how to ride in case you need to go into town and the wagon isn't here." He held out the pair of denim pants. "It'll be easier for you if you don't have to worry about your skirts and petticoats getting in the way."

Josie laughed but didn't reach out to take them. "I'm not putting on your pants," she sputtered. "Why, what will people think?"

"They're not my pants," he told her. "They're Nora's."

Josie's eyes widened. Nora wore pants? She'd never seen Nora in anything but proper women's wear, but was it possible most women in the west wore pants sometimes?

"They might not fit you properly, but ..." His gaze slid slowly from her head to her toes, and a slow heat built inside her. "You're not much different than Nora is."

"What will people think?" she repeated.

"What people are those?" he asked. "There's just us here today. Nobody will see you."

Josie still wasn't convinced, but she didn't want to argue. "If you're sure ..."

"I am."

With a sigh of resignation, she hung the dish towel on a hook and took the pants. "I never thought I'd live to see the day I'd be wearing men's clothes ..." she muttered as she left the kitchen and went upstairs to change.

Within a few minutes, she was surveying her reflection in the mirror. Nora was thinner than she was, so the pants fit snugly around her waist and her backside. She turned sideways, taking note of how the pants clung to her hips and emphasized her legs. The stiff fabric rubbed against her inner thighs, which wasn't overly pleasant, but at the same time, she did find wearing the pants quite freeing. It was a change to not have to worry about petticoats and skirts getting caught in anything.

"Are you ready yet?" Cooper's voice called out from the bottom of the stairs.

With one last look in the mirror, she sucked in a deep breath and joined him downstairs.

He grinned. "I think I like seeing you in those," he said, doing his best to wiggle his eyebrows suggestively while his gaze raked over her.

His obvious approval as he studied her caused her veins to tingle, and she tamped it down. "Don't get used to it," she told him. "I'll only wear these when we're alone."

"Then I'll be sure to look at you a lot today while you have them on."

She blushed. "Then I'll be sure to walk behind you so you can't."

"You'd refuse me that little bit of pleasure ..." he said with a chuckle.

She opened the door and stood behind the door so she was half-hidden. He was teasing her, but she didn't mind. In fact, if she was being completely honest with herself, she actually found that his flirtatious remarks excited her. She felt desirable, something she'd never felt before, and it was a heady feeling. She couldn't let him see how his words affected her, though. Forcing herself to be stern, she gave him a withering look. "Are you going to teach me to ride or not?"

Gold, orange and pink streaks painted the sky. Lately, it had become a habit to sit on the porch in the evenings with Josie and watch the sun set behind the mountains. Cooper never tired of the view, and it seemed Josie felt the same way.

He slid a glance in her direction. Her eyes glittered in the lantern light and her cheeks were flushed from the heat, but it only made her even prettier than she already was.

Once she'd gotten past her initial fear of the mare he'd saddled for her, she'd taken to riding as if she'd been riding all her life.

"Thank you for today," she said softly, the lilt of her voice washing over him like sweet honey. "I enjoyed it."

He looked over at her, at the way the last rays of daylight caught the golden tones in her hair and the sparkle in her eyes.

"I'm glad," he replied. "I liked showing you the ranch." They'd ridden until they'd reached the river that formed the boundary between his ranch and the Grimsby ranch. They'd dismounted there to let the horses drink and spent an hour resting under a tree, talking about nothing ... and everything.

He couldn't remember ever feeling so relaxed in the company of another person, especially a woman.

"Your ranch is beautiful. All of it."

"Our ranch," he pointed out.

She grinned. "*Our ranch* is the most beautiful ranch ever."

"Even the brambles?" he teased.

She'd gotten her leg tangled in some brambles when she was wandering while the horses were resting during their ride that afternoon. Luckily, the heavy pants she'd been wearing had prevented her from being hurt. "Even the brambles."

They sat in comfortable silence until night fell and the stars twinkled in the clear sky above.

"Have you ever wished on a star, Cooper?" Josie asked.

"No. Have you?"

"Once. I wished my parents would come back for me, but that didn't happen."

"I'm sorry."

"Maybe they weren't meant to come back, so that I stayed at the orphanage, and I eventually came here."

Cooper thought about that for a while. He was pleased that she was happy to be here, pleased that they could spend their evenings sitting quietly together, and their nights making love.

He wouldn't let himself love her, but he was pretty sure he liked her a whole lot, and he was content with that.

He reached out and took her hand. He brought it to his lips and lightly kissed it. "Then I'm glad your wish didn't come true."

~

Andy had been fussing all morning, but finally, he'd fallen asleep upstairs. He was exhausted from the trip to see his grandparents, and he'd slept more than usual since he and Drew arrived home late three days before.

Josie poured herself a cup of coffee and sat down at the kitchen table to write a long-overdue letter to Sally.

. . .

Dear Sally,
   I have so much to tell you ...

She continued to write, pouring out the details of everything that had happened since she left Chicago. Everything except her feelings for Cooper. She couldn't find the right words to explain the sense of peace and contentment she'd found, and the way her feelings for Cooper were growing stronger every day. She knew that if only he loved her ... and if she could give him a child of his own ... her life would be perfect.

She had just sealed the envelope when she heard a knock at the door.

Setting the pen on the blotting paper, she hurried to the door and opened it. She was thrilled to see Nora standing on the porch, a plate covered in a checkered cloth in her hands.

"Come in, come in," Josie said excitedly. "It's so good to see you. Cooper has been teaching me to ride so I could come to visit you, but I've only had one lesson so I'm not good enough to go off on my own yet."

For the next two hours, the ladies drank tea and ate the cinnamon bread Nora had brought with her.

"There's a dance in town on Saturday night," Nora told her. "Lewis and I are going, and you have to persuade Cooper to take you. It'll be fun. He'll come up with a dozen excuses why he can't go, but if he knows you really want to go, he'll give in. It'll be fun."

"I've never been to a dance," she said, "but it would be

nice to get away from the ranch for a few hours. Not that I'm complaining. I love being here more every day—"

"And what about my brother?" Nora's eyes twinkled. "Are you growing to like him more every day, too?"

Nora seemed to be able to read her thoughts. For days now, Josie had been examining her feelings for Cooper. She'd never known what it was like to love or be loved, so she wasn't sure. All she knew was that she missed him when he was away and that every minute she was with him, she was happier than she'd ever thought possible.

And when he touched her, or kissed her ... her body seemed to have a mind of its own.

Was it love? And if it was, what was she going to do about it?

She was fairly sure Cooper liked her, but she was positive he didn't love her. She was sure of that. He treated her well, and he was always gentle with her, but that didn't mean he loved her.

She couldn't bring herself to voice her thoughts to Nora, though. Nora and Lewis were so much in love, and even though Josie fought it, she was envious. She wanted the same kind of relationship they had.

Stop it! she chided herself. She should be thankful for the life she had instead of coveting things that were impossible.

"I like him and I think he likes me, so we're content," she said.

Suddenly, the door opened and Cooper strode in.

After giving his sister a hug, he sat with them at the table, catching up on the latest news.

"So you'll be bringing Josie to the dance on Saturday, won't you?"

"Dance? Oh … yeah … I did see something about it."

"So we'll see you then?" she asked.

"If Josie would like to go, I don't mind," he replied.

Nora's eyes widened. "You're not going to argue?" Turning to Josie, she laughed. "What have you done to him?"

Josie shook her head. The relationship Cooper and Nora had was special. She could see that, even when they were bickering, it was done with love and respect.

"Do you want to go?" Cooper asked Josie.

Mrs. Norton had made sure all the children learned to dance, at least enough not to embarrass themselves, but she'd never really mastered the skill. Still, it would be nice to have an evening away from the ranch. She nodded. "I'd like to, very much."

"Okay then," he said, turning his attention to Nora. "We'll see you there."

He got up and put his hat back on his head. "Drew and I are heading out to the north pasture so I'll be a bit late for supper. That's what I came in to tell you. Now you'll have more time to visit, so it all works out."

"That's fine," Josie replied with a smile.

He turned and left them. As soon as the front door closed, Nora grinned. "He loves you."

Josie felt a flush rising to her cheeks. "What? That's ridiculous."

"Oh, it's not ridiculous at all. I know my brother. That's the only reason I can think of why he'd agree to go to a dance without any argument at all." She nodded her head. "Yes, I'm right. Mark my words. He might not know it yet, but he loves you. No question about it. Now, it's getting late and I have to get back."

Nora collected her things and made her way outside. Josie went with her and stood beside the buggy until she was ready to leave. "Thank you so much for coming," Josie said. "I've really enjoyed our visit, and I hope we can do it again soon."

"I'll see you on Saturday night," Nora reminded her, then with a wave, she set off.

Josie watched her go, her excitement building. She'd never been to a real dance, and she couldn't wait.

As she went back inside and started clearing the table, Nora's words echoed in her mind.

He loves you.

She sighed. If only that was true …

CHAPTER 8

"*D*o you want to help me fix the well, Andy?"

Josie had noticed the past few times she'd collected water that the wall was beginning to crumble.

She'd thought about mentioning it to Cooper, but he and Drew were always so busy she decided against adding more to their workload, especially since she was confident she could repair it herself. The same thing had happened at the orphanage a few times, and Hank had taught her how to make sure she had the right mixture of mud and straw. If the soil here had a clay base, she could take care of it.

Andy looked up from the wooden train he was rolling on the floor and nodded. "What'cha gonna do?"

Josie opened the door and Andy hurried outside and down the steps. He raced to the well. Josie joined him and crouched down. "See here?" she asked, pointing at the dried muddy material holding the wall of the well together. "The cement is crumbling and the rocks will fall out soon if we don't fix it."

"How you gonna fix it?"

"We need to put more mud between the rocks," she said. Turning the handle, she raised the bucket out of the well and poured a little water on the ground beside them. Then she reached down and scooped up a handful of soil. She formed it into a ball and smiled. "Perfect."

Andy copied her, grinning. "I like to play in mud." Then his smile disappeared. "Papa will get mad."

"No, he won't," Josie said with a chuckle. "He's going to be so proud of you for helping me fix it. Now we need some straw."

"I can get it," Andy announced, dropping the mud ball and racing toward the barn. Josie followed behind him and by the time she reached the barn door, he'd already gathered an armful of straw from the floor.

"Good work, Andy," Josie said. "I'll get some, too, and then we'll be ready."

While Andy waited for her, Josie picked up as much straw as she could carry. They likely wouldn't need it all, but it would save them another trip to the barn.

"We need to break the straw into smaller pieces," Josie told Andy as they walked back to the well. "Can you help me do that?"

Andy nodded, and a minute or two later, they had a pile of small pieces of straw.

"Now we have to get as many little stones out of the dirt as we can, okay?"

Andy dug his small fingers into the dirt, picking out

the stones and tossing them into a heap beside him until Josie estimated they had enough.

Josie grinned. "Now we have fun." Adding water to the dirt, she dug her hands in and began mixing.

"We have fun," Andy repeated, sinking his hands into the mud and swirling it.

"Toss in some straw, Andy," Josie told him.

Andy picked up some straw and threw it. Most of it hit Josie, but she didn't mind. Soon, they were both covered in straw and mud, and giggling.

Josie took a handful of the mud and slapped it on the wall of the well, tucking it into the spaces between the rocks. "Your turn."

They were almost finished when the sound of hoof-beats filled the air. Josie looked up to see Cooper astride his horse, watching them. "What in Heaven's name are you two doing?"

"Fixing the well," Josie replied with a smile.

Cooper's brows drew together. "You couldn't wait for me to fix it?"

By the tone of his voice, it was obvious he didn't approve, although she had no idea why he'd object. She was helping him, after all. "Didn't see any reason to."

"You need to have the right mix—"

"I know that," she replied bluntly. "I fixed the well at the orphanage several times. The soil here is perfect."

He didn't answer for a few minutes. His gaze settled on Andy happily slapping mud on the wall. Finally, he turned his attention back to Josie. "I don't need you to do my chores, you know."

Suddenly, she understood. It wasn't what she was doing that bothered him, but that he felt she was criticizing him for not doing the work himself. "I know that. I'm only trying to help. Isn't that what a wife is supposed to do?"

He didn't answer. With a flick of the reins, he rode away in the direction of the barn and disappeared inside.

Josie watched him go, the pleasure she'd felt at easing his workload gone.

Cooper heaved a coil of thick rope onto his shoulder and strode across the yard toward the well. He couldn't stop his gaze from drifting to the rocks that Josie had repaired.

He smiled. The woman was remarkable, never expecting him to do anything she could do herself.

She was always willing—no, she was always eager—to do what he considered man's work, and she made a point of tackling these chores when he wasn't around to stop her.

He'd been annoyed, though, when he'd seen her and Andy fixing the well. That was his job, not hers. For a while, he'd felt as if he wasn't working hard enough, that she thought she had to do his work for him, too.

Then he'd come to his senses and apologized. She'd forgiven him immediately, as if she'd understood.

When he'd been watching her work the day before,

he'd noticed the rope holding the bucket was frayed, and he was surprised it hadn't worn through altogether.

He was also surprised she hadn't already fixed the rope herself. He'd asked her about it after supper the night before. She'd told him she couldn't do it because she didn't think she could tighten the knot enough. Then she'd reminded him she only attempted man's work—and she'd emphasized those words—when she was sure she was capable.

He pulled the bucket out of the well and set it on the ground, then took a knife out of its sheath and cut through the knot tied around the handle. As he cut through the other knot and replaced the rope, his thoughts strayed back to his sister's visit.

Dancing! As soon as Nora had mentioned it, he'd been all set to tell her he didn't have time to go into town. He needed to clear brush, fix one of the fence posts a bull had rammed a few days ago before it knocked it down completely. And he still hadn't gotten around to fixing the leak on the roof of the chicken coop. The chickens were none too happy when they got wet but luckily, they hadn't had a bad storm for a while.

But then he'd met Josie's gaze, her eyes bright with excitement, and he hadn't been able to say no. Nora had obviously taught her well, he mused. Did that mean he wouldn't ever be able to say no to her the way he never could to his sister?

What had gotten into him? He'd thought he'd managed to get away from a woman running his life when Nora married Lewis. He muttered a soft curse. Looked like he'd just traded one woman who could wrap him around her little finger for another.

With Nora, it made sense. She was his sister and he loved her. But Josie? What gave Josie the power to make him want to give her whatever she asked for. Hell, she hadn't even had to ask for anything. One look from those bright whisky-colored eyes and he'd been ready to give her the moon if she wanted it.

With one last tug on the rope, he set the bucket on the side of the well and gathered up the rotting rope and headed to the field behind the barn where he threw it in the burn pile. He made a mental note to burn the trash the next time the wind was blowing away from the house.

Hearing a sound coming from behind him, he turned in time to see Josie going up the porch stairs. She caught his gaze and smiled at him, then disappeared inside the house.

What was it about her that made him practically fall over himself to give her everything she wanted without her even asking? He still didn't have an answer by the time he'd finished his chores and he washed up for supper.

Coldwater Creek's meeting hall was crowded by the time Josie and Cooper found an empty spot to leave the wagon near the edge of town that Saturday night.

Josie could barely contain her excitement, especially

when Cooper lifted her out of the wagon and held her a few moments longer than he had to.

"You look really pretty tonight, Josie," he said.

Her heartbeat fluttered. She'd been sewing furiously all week to finish the pale green dress she'd started three weeks before. It fit perfectly. She'd lost weight since she arrived in Coldwater Creek and it emphasized her new curves. She'd taken extra pains with her hair, and pinching her cheeks and adding a touch of lip rouge made her look older than her years, a look she was happy about.

It seemed Cooper was happy about it, too, she thought as he tucked her hand beneath his elbow and they approached the hall.

Lanterns brightened the boardwalk and the hall. Inside, dancers crowded the floor, the music loud. Josie paused at the entrance, watching, suddenly feeling very intimidated. She'd learned how to waltz, but not with the ease and skill of those twirling around the room.

Her spirits sank. She'd been looking forward to this night all week, and now … she just wanted to go home.

"Do you want to dance?" Cooper's voice whispered in her ear.

She shook her head. No, she didn't want to make a fool of herself.

Confusion crossed his face. "I thought …" He paused, peered at her. "Do you know how to dance?"

"Yes … no … well, yes … but not enough to join them." Her gaze slid to one couple gliding across the floor.

"Me either, but I'm willing to give it a try if you are." He held out his hand and smiled at her. She'd never been held in his arms other than when they were making love, and the temptation was too great to deny.

Taking his hand, she let him lead her onto the dance floor. "Ready?"

She nodded, and they began to move. She grinned when she heard him counting—one, two, three, one, two, three, one, two, three—as he led her around the floor. She didn't care. His warm hand splayed on her back and the woodsy scent of his shaving cream filled her nose. The rest of the dancers faded away until there was just her ... in Cooper's arms, moving as if they were floating on air.

All too soon, the music stopped. Josie looked up at him, the man she loved. Somehow, during the song, the truth had hit her. She loved him. Loved him with every cell in her body.

"What's wrong?" he asked. "You suddenly look so serious."

"What ... oh ... nothing ... nothing at all." She sent him a smile she hoped would satisfy him.

"Did I step on your toes?"

"No." She grinned. "Well ... only once or twice."

"Sorry. I've been told I do that sometimes," he went on. "In fact, one time my dancing partner walked off and danced with somebody else because she said I'd stepped on her toes so much I'd flattened them."

He was smiling while he told her about it, so Josie didn't bother to squash the laughter bubbling up inside her. "I actually tripped my partner once. He was one of the taller boys in the orphanage, and when he fell, he crashed into a table and knocked over a vase of flowers."

"I'm guessing he didn't ask you to dance again," Cooper commented.

"You're right."

They were both still laughing when Drew wandered over to stand beside them. "Looks like you two are having a good time," he said.

"I am," Josie replied.

"Can I have the next dance?" he asked Josie, then turned to Cooper. "You don't mind, do you?"

Josie glanced at Cooper's face. His smile had faded, and for a split second, he seemed ... annoyed. Why, she couldn't say, and the expression in his eyes disappeared so quickly she wondered if she'd imagined it. "Not a bit."

Between Drew, Cooper and a few of their friends who politely invited her to dance with them, Josie barely sat down. She couldn't remember when she'd enjoyed herself so much.

"Thank you so much for tonight," she said softly when they were on their way back to the ranch. Drew had gone to fetch Andy from Mrs. Dawson, who'd agreed to watch him for the evening.

Cooper glanced over at her. "I'm glad you had a good time," he said, reaching over and squeezing her hand. "I've never been much for socializing, but maybe it's time we did a bit more of it."

Knowing they'd be traveling home after nightfall, he'd rigged a lantern to light their way. He sent a smile in

Josie's direction, noticing how her eyes were sparkling and her hair glistened in the glow of the lantern.

She really was pretty, and what made her even prettier was the fact that she didn't even realize it.

"Did you enjoy it?" she asked him.

Surprisingly, he had enjoyed himself. He rarely took time away from the ranch to catch up with the latest news, or to even talk business with the other ranchers in the area. He'd always counted on Drew to find out any information he might need to know.

Tonight was the first time in quite a while he'd gotten together with other men to share a drink. He hadn't been able to put Josie out of his mind, though, and he'd caught himself watching her while she socialized with the other ladies.

But most of all, he'd enjoyed dancing with her. Even though they'd made love, he'd never really just held her in his arms before for no reason.

Tonight, when his mind wasn't on anything but the way she moved against him as they danced, he'd noticed she was a little thinner now than when she first arrived, and that bothered him. She worked hard. Was she working too hard? After all, she wasn't used to the constant work of being a rancher's wife. And if she got sick because of it … He didn't even want to think about that possibility.

~

Wind howled and driving rain battered the house. Inside, Josie was at the table eating scrambled eggs and bacon, while Andy was stuffing "soldiers"—buttered bread sliced into narrow strips—into the yolk of a boiled egg.

"Where's Papa and Uncle Cooper?" Andy asked, then plopped an egg-soaked soldier into his mouth. "When they coming back?"

That was a good question, Josie thought. They'd been gone since the evening before, and she'd spent the entire night waiting for them, trying not to worry.

Earlier, she'd gone out to the barn to milk the cow since they hadn't come back. "I don't know, Andy," she replied. "Some of the cows got caught in the mud so they're trying to get them out."

"Why did the cows go in the mud?" Andy interrupted. "Papa doesn't like it when I go in the mud."

"I don't know." Josie got up and took her plate to the washbasin and slid it into the soapy water. "Now finish your breakfast."

She should go out and collect the eggs, she supposed. She hated the thought of venturing outside, but it didn't look like the rain was going to let up any time soon, and she needed eggs to bake the cookies she planned to take to the sewing bee she'd been invited to the next day.

Sheets of rain teemed down from a slate-grey sky and tree branches bowed from the force of the wind.

I won't melt in a little rain, she assured herself, tugging on a slicker and boots. "I'll just be a few minutes," she said to Andy as she picked up the egg basket and opened the door.

Rain pelted her like tiny daggers as she crossed the yard. Even over the sound of the wind howling, she could hear the chickens squawking. What was wrong with them?

As soon as she reached the henhouse, she saw what the ruckus was about. Rain had seeped through a leak in the roof and flooded it.

Since they only had a few chickens, there was only one row of roosts, set just above the ground. They were already practically under water, and the chickens were flapping wildly, squawking their annoyance as they tried to escape.

Apparently chickens did not like to get wet and the problem was only going to get worse if she didn't do something about it. There was no way of knowing when Cooper and Drew would get back to fix the roof, so it was up to her.

She knew what to do, but she didn't relish the thought of climbing a ladder in this weather. Still, she had no choice. She didn't know if it was possible, but if it was, she didn't want to be responsible for letting the chickens drown.

Going back into the house, she took Andy out to the porch so that she could keep an eye on him while she fixed the roof. "Do not leave the porch, Andy," she told him. "Promise?"

He nodded solemnly.

Josie hurried to the barn, hoping she'd be able to find something to seal the leak, at least temporarily. The lack of light inside the barn made it hard to see, but she found a pile of shingles in the corner, probably left over from the roof Cooper had been fixing the day she'd arrived.

A soft smile tugged at her lips as the memory washed over her. He'd been so angry that day. And now … how things had changed.

Since she wasn't sure how big the hole in the roof was, she gathered up a few shingles, a hammer and nails. After taking them back to the henhouse and setting them on top of the small lean-to attached to it, she went back to the barn to get the ladder, half-dragging it through the muddy yard.

She wiped the rain and her hair out of her eyes and struggled to rest the ladder against the side of the henhouse. Depositing a few nails and the head of the hammer in her pocket, she tucked a shingle under her arm and put her foot on the first rung.

The ladder shifted, and her heart tumbled in her chest. Another rung. So far so good.

She'd almost reached the roof when the ladder slowly began to slide sideways. Panic surged through her. The shingle under her arm forgotten, she reached out, trying to catch hold of something … anything. All she grabbed was air.

The ladder toppled, and Josie fell. Cold, wet mud met her, and pain exploded in her head.

Then the world went black.

∾

Cooper was exhausted, but he and Drew had managed to rescue at least a dozen calves from a mudhole near the river, and moved more than fifty head of cattle to a pasture on a rise, away from the worst of the flooding.

All he wanted now was food and sleep. Knowing Josie, she'd welcome him home with a smile, and have a hot meal keeping warm for them.

The rain had finally stopped, but the sky was still lead gray, with no sign of sunshine anytime soon.

"I'll milk the cow if you take care of the horses," Cooper said to Drew as they rode across the fields toward the ranch house.

Drew nodded. "Sounds fair. Doesn't look like we'll get much else done today."

They rode in silence until the house came into view. There was no smoke coming from the chimney, no lantern light glowing in the windows.

Strange, Cooper thought.

"What's that?" Drew asked, squinting into the dim light.

Cooper followed his gaze. Something was resting against the door, something unrecognizable. Suddenly, it moved.

"It's Andy!" Drew sputtered. "What's Andy doing sitting on the porch? Where's Josie?"

"Something's wrong," Cooper said quietly, his heart-beat racing. Tension slithered up his spine. Urging his horse to a gallop, he raced toward the house, Drew right behind him.

Andy was sitting cross-legged on the porch. He was soaked but otherwise looked unharmed.

Both men dismounted. Drew bounded up the steps and picked Drew up, hugging him to his chest. "What are you doing sitting out here, Andy?" Drew asked. "Where's Auntie Josie?"

Andy pointed toward the side of the house. "She's sleeping."

Fear ... breath-stealing fear ... exploded in his chest. "Sleeping? What do you mean, she's sleeping? Where?"

"With the chickens," Andy replied. "She went to get eggs, and fell asleep with the chickens."

Cooper was already racing toward the henhouse, his heart in his throat when he saw the ladder lying on the ground, and Josie in a heap beside it.

Sliding in the mud, he dropped to his knees at her side. Was she breathing? If she wasn't ... He couldn't bring himself to even think about it! His chest squeezed so tight he could barely draw a breath, and for a few moments, he was worried he might be physically sick. She couldn't be ... She just couldn't.

Because he loved her. Somehow he'd fallen in love with her and he'd been too stupid and ornery to realize it until now. Now, when he might not get the chance to tell her.

He reached under her and drew her close to him. She was so cold! "Josie! Josie! Come on, Josie. Open your eyes," he croaked past the lump of fear in his throat.

For what seemed like hours, she didn't move. Finally, her eyelids flickered open, then closed again.

As if a weight had been lifted, he sucked in a breath. She was alive! She might be badly injured, but she was alive. "Drew! Ride into town and get the doc! Tell him we need him right now!"

He only hoped he wasn't too late!

CHAPTER 9

*J*osie couldn't remember ever being so cold!

A giant drum like she'd seen in the 4th of July parade the year before was pounding in her head, making her stomach roil.

She tried to move, but every muscle screamed in protest. She must still be alive to hurt so badly, she reasoned, and as long as she stayed perfectly still, only her head felt as if it was about to explode with every beat of her heart.

"Josie?"

She recognized Cooper's voice, felt his arm slide under her and draw her against the hard wall of his chest. The movements were agonizing, but she didn't even have the strength to cry out.

His warmth seeped into her and the scent of leather reached her nose as he cocooned her against him with his duster.

"Josie, open your eyes, honey." Cooper's voice sounded strange, almost panicked.

Later, she thought. She'd open them later, once she dared to do more than breathe.

His voice filtered through the hammering in her head. "Oh, God, you can't die. Not now!"

Oh, how she just wanted to be warm again. And to sleep.

She forced her eyelids to open. Even though there was no sunshine, the light stabbed them so she closed them again.

"That's it," he whispered in her ear, his hot breath warming her neck. "You're going to be fine. Drew went to fetch the doc. You'll be fine."

She felt Cooper lifting her, her body jarring. She clenched her teeth against the pain. "I'll be … fine …" she murmured as blackness claimed her again.

Soft lamplight illuminated the room when Josie woke and opened her eyes. She still had a headache, and she was sure she'd be bruised and achy for a few days, but she was warm, and she was hungry.

The door opened and Cooper walked in. He grinned when he saw she was awake, and set the basin he was carrying on the nightstand. Sliding into the chair beside the bed, he reached out and took her hand. "How are you feeling?"

"Better," she croaked through the dryness in her throat. "Thirsty."

Cooper poured a glass of water from the pitcher on the bureau and supported her while she took a few sips. Then he gently laid her head back on the pillow.

"Are you sure?"

"Positive."

"You have no idea how scared I was when I saw you lying there on the ground, not moving."

"It was really cold … and wet," she commented with a small smile.

"But you're really feeling better."

She nodded.

His smile disappeared and a frown creased his forehead. "Good. Then, would you like to tell me what the hell you were thinking? You could have broken your neck. What were you doing up there?"

Why was he so angry? He wasn't the one who'd fallen off the roof. "Fixing the hole in the roof," she explained. "The chickens were going to drown—"

"They were not going to drown," he contradicted. "There's a section in the back they could have roosted on until the rain stopped. You've probably just never noticed it before."

"How was I to know that?" she asked. "I was trying to help."

"Fixing a roof is a man's job," he went on. "You could have broken your neck."

Even though she was sore and her head was pounding, her temper surged. "And a man couldn't break his neck falling off a ladder?"

He ignored her question. "You had no business even climbing a ladder without somebody there to hold it steady for you."

"You mean like you had the day I got here," she pointed out. "I don't recall seeing anyone steadying the ladder for you."

"That's different—"

She shifted her position, grimacing as her body protested. She glared at him. "How is it different?"

"It ... it just is."

He turned his back on her and paced to the other end of the room before turning back to spear her with his dark eyes. "I don't want you taking risks like that!"

"I didn't really think I was taking a risk," she put in. "I've climbed ladders so many times ..."

"All it takes is one slip."

"I know that now."

"We found Andy sitting on the porch. Alone. He could have wandered off, could have gotten hurt."

Guilt surged through Josie. In her defense, she hadn't thought she'd have an accident, but that really was no excuse. She shouldn't have done what she did, and if anything had happened to Andy because of her, she never would have been able to live with herself. Tears burned her eyes. "You're right ... I'm so sorry ..."

"Just promise me you won't do anything like that again. Leave man's work to the men."

For a few moments, she considered it, then shook her

head even though the pain ricocheting through it at the movement made her regret it. But she couldn't be somebody she wasn't, not even for Cooper. "I can't do that," she said.

"I ... I don't want to lose you."

Josie's anger fizzled out and warmth spread through her veins. "You're not going to lose me. I will promise you I won't do anything that could be dangerous when I'm alone. If that's not good enough—"

"That's all I ask." Cooper perched on the edge of the straight-backed chair beside the bed. Reaching out, he buried her hand between his. "Josie, I can't have you taking chances ... I can't risk something happening to you ..."

"I'm sure somebody else can look after Andy just as well as I can."

"Andy?"

"Yes ... you pointed out that I was responsible for him—"

Cooper began to laugh, the booming sound filling the room.

Her head pound even harder. "Please stop!" she wailed.

His laughter died. "I'm sorry," he said. "You think that's the only reason I worry about you getting yourself killed?"

"What other reason could there be?"

"Maybe that ... that I love you. That's why," he snapped.

She must be hearing things. Yes, she thought, her

head injury was making her hallucinate. "What did you say?"

"I love you," he repeated. "I didn't realize it until today. When I saw you lying on the ground, my insides felt like they were being ripped into a million pieces. I was terrified you were dead. Thank God you were just knocked out. Not that a concussion is a good thing, but—"

"I have a concussion?"

"That's what the doc says."

""Would that affect my hearing and understanding?"

"I don't know. Why?"

"Because I thought I heard you say you loved me, but since I do have a concussion, I could have imagined it."

"You didn't."

"You really love me?"

He nodded. "I never figured on loving anybody, but somehow when I wasn't looking, I fell in love with you."

Tears filled Josie's eyes and streamed down her face, the scrape on her cheek stinging from the salt in her tears. "You did?"

"I was so content with my life before you came along," he said a long heartbeat later. "I didn't want anything else, especially a woman who'd make me want to do things like go dancing, or sit quietly beside her on a porch in the evenings watching the sun go down. Or who'd make me think about having a family of my own."

"And now?"

"Now I know how empty it really was. You made me

want to do all those things and more just to see you smile."

Josie smiled, her love for Cooper filling her, overpowering the pain in her body. Then she laughed. The pain in her head worsened, but she didn't care.

"You think it's funny that I'm at your mercy?" he asked.

She shook her head, then groaned at the movement. "It is, because we've wasted so much time."

"What do you mean?"

"I mean that I love you, too. I've loved you almost since the day I got here," she replied as she struggled to a sitting position and tugged at his hand.

"Is that so?"

"It is." She patted a spot in the bed beside her. "Now come here."

Accepting her invitation, he climbed into the bed with her and wrapped his arms around her. His lips met hers and he kissed her soundly until she was breathless and her headache was forgotten.

Josie gazed up at him and smiled. "I was so afraid when Mrs. Norton told me I had to leave the orphanage. I had no home, no family to go to, and I decided coming west couldn't be any worse than staying in Chicago. I didn't know it was going to bring me more happiness than I ever thought possible."

He kissed her again. "There is one thing ..."

Her forehead wrinkled in a frown. "What is it?"

"Now that I know you feel the same way about me that I do about you, it would be really easy to spend my days right here," he said, "but I need to get the chores done and you need to rest. You do have that concussion, remember?"

"Tell me again that you love me."

Cooper shifted and cupped her face in his hands. His gaze met hers. "I love you, Mrs. Thompson. I love you. I love you. I love you."

Josie grinned. "Well, since I do have a concussion and it's possible I'll forget, you might have to remind me regularly."

He leaned over and kissed her again. "If it'll make you happy, I'll tell you every day for the rest of my life."

She snuggled closer, her heart swelling with love. Her body was bruised and scraped and her head ached, but she'd never been happier. Gazing up at him, she smiled. Happiness filled her to overflowing. "It will."

"Then that's how it'll be."

EPILOGUE

*J*osie and Cooper stood on the front porch
and waved as Nora and Lewis drove away,
the light from the lantern Lewis had hung
on their wagon swaying in the darkness.

Cooper took Josie's hand and brought it to his lips.
"That was the best Thanksgiving I've ever had," he said
softly.

Josie nodded in agreement. She'd prayed that one day,
she'd have a family of her own, and this day, with Cooper
—and with Drew and Andy, and Nora and Lewis, had
been one of the best days of her life. She had so much to
be thankful for.

Josie looked up at her husband, her heart filled with
love for this man, and for the family she now had. Drew
and Andy still spent much of their time with her and
Cooper. Nora was expecting a baby very soon, and Josie

was almost sure Nora's child would have a playmate within a few months.

Josie couldn't remember ever being happier, and it was all thanks to Nora. She'd never forget that, and gave thanks for her friend every day.

"What are you smiling at?" Cooper asked, gazing down at her.

She tucked her hand beneath Cooper's elbow and grinned up at him. "Just thinking how lucky I am."

He squeezed her hand. "I'm the lucky one. I didn't even know I was missing something in my life until you showed me."

"I knew I was missing something," she said softly. "I didn't know I'd find it here. With you."

She gazed up at her husband, the man she loved. Her life had begun the day she arrived in Coldwater Creek, and she couldn't wait to spend the rest of it right here. With Cooper and the family she'd always dreamed of.

SALLY, the second book in the Brides of Coldwater Creek series, is ready for you to read next.

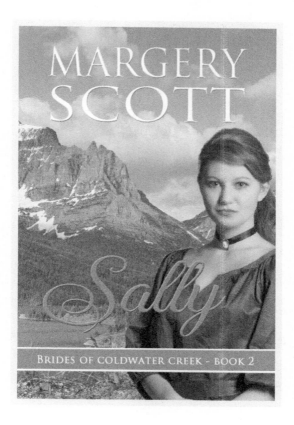

Can a man without a future and a woman with a past build a family? Or will the past destroy any chance of a future together?

GET YOUR COPY NOW!

ABOUT THE AUTHOR

Margery Scott is the author of more than thirty novels, novellas and short stories in various genres. Although she grew up as far away from the old west as possible, Margery has always admired the men and women who settled the untamed land west of the Mississippi. Glued to TV westerns like Maverick, Rawhide and Gunsmoke, and reading stories of Annie Oakley, Roy Rogers and Rin Tin Tin, it was only natural that when she started writing, she wrote what she loved to watch and read. She now lives on a lake in Canada with her husband, and when she's not writing or travelling in search of the perfect setting for her next novel, you can usually find her wielding a pair of knitting needles or a pool cue.

Website: www.margeryscott.com
Email: margery@margeryscott.com

Follow Margery on:
Facebook: www.facebook.com/AuthorMargeryScott
Twitter: www.twitter.com/margeryscott
Bookbub: www.bookbub.com/authors/margery-scott
Instagram: www.instagram.com/margeryscott48

Made in the USA
Monee, IL
19 September 2022

14269401R10080